ULTIMATE ENDING

BOOK 3

THE SHIP
AT THE
EDGE OF TIME

Check out the full

ULTIMATE ENDING BOOKS

Series:

TREASURES OF THE FORGOTTEN CITY

THE HOUSE ON HOLLOW HILL

THE SHIP AT THE EDGE OF TIME

ENIGMA AT THE GREENSBORO ZOO

THE SECRET OF THE AURORA HOTEL

THE STRANGE PHYSICS OF THE HEIDELBERG LABORATORY

THE TOWER OF NEVER THERE

Cover design by Xia Taptara www.xiataptara.com

Internal artwork by Romeo Boldador livyx.deviantart.com

Enjoyed this book? Please take the time to leave a review on Amazon.

Dedicated to all the future Masters of Time and Space,
whomever they may be.

Welcome to **Ultimate Ending,**
where YOU choose the story!

That's right – everything that happens in this book is a result of
decisions YOU make. So choose wisely!

But also be careful. Throughout this book you'll find tricks and traps,
trials and tribulations! Most you can avoid with common sense and a
logical approach to problem solving. Others will require a little bit of luck.
Having a coin handy, or a pair of dice, will make your adventure even more
fun. So grab em' if you got em'!

Along the way you'll also find tips, clues, and even items that can help
you in your quest. You'll meet people. Pick stuff up. Taking note of these
things is often important, so while you're gathering your courage, you
might also want to grab yourself a pencil and a sheet of paper.

Keep in mind, there are *many* ways to end the story. Some conclusions
are good... some not so good.
Some of them are even great!
But remember:

There is only *ONE*

ULTIMATE
ENDING!

THE SHIP AT THE EDGE OF TIME

Welcome to Outer Space!

The year is 2260, and the solar system has long been colonized by the Earth World Coalition and the Mars-Jupiter Alliance. Space thrives with ships of all shapes and sizes – building, exploring, and discovering.

You are Lt. Colonel ANDON MERCER, space marine. Together with first mate and co-pilot SERENA VALENTINE, the two of you fly the Kestrel, a Codec-class scout ship tasked with patrolling the outer edges of known space. Every day is the same: quiet, routine. Every day up until now.

"Lieutenant Colonel," a voice calls from inside your helmet. "This is Commodore Garriott of the EWC Blackthorne."

It takes you less than a second to open a channel. "I read you Commodore. Go ahead."

"A ship has appeared on the outer edge of the belt," he tells you. "Unknown origin. All attempts to hail it have failed, and our scans are coming up empty." The Commodore pauses. "Right now, you're closest."

A new waypoint blinks to life on your screen. He's right. It's not far at all. "Orders?"

"Your orders are to intercept, board and investigate," the Commodore continues. "At least until we get there."

"Roger that," you reply. Your terminal rapidly begins filling with information as Serena plots your newly-adjusted course. "Anything else, sir?"

"Yes, Lieutenant Colonel. Use caution."

"Affirmative."

In no time at all you're accelerating past cruise velocity, speeding through space on a direct intercept for the derelict ship. Over the rim of your faceshield you shoot Serena a sideways glance.

"Ready for this?" you ask.

"Are you kidding?" she smirks back. "Been waiting forever."

8

At full thrust it doesn't take long to reach the edge of the asteroid belt. You squint through the blackness of the Kestrel's viewport and watch as the strange, derelict ship floats into view.

"One of ours?" you ask.

"Hard to say," Serena replies. "It's certainly not a design I've ever seen. And it's transmitting on a totally unknown transponder code."

Except for a few distant running lights the ship appears dark and silent. Your console tells you two things: it's moving at a very high rate of speed, and it's heading directly for Earth.

"Hail it."

"I've been hailing it for ten minutes," Serena tells you. "No response."

You look down again at your console, which reads green across the board. Although much larger than the Kestrel, the strange vessel seems bent on ignoring you. For right now at least, it poses no discernible threat.

"Coming around."

It takes some maneuvering, but you manage to slingshot alongside the sleek, dark ship. As you get closer you can see that it's definitely Earth-made. There's a name stenciled across the bow:

DAUNTLESS

Serena brings you out of your trance with a tap on the shoulder. She points one finger to an external airlock.

"Any other ideas?" you ask.

"Not offhand."

"Fine then. Let's go."

10

"Docking procedure initiated," you tell your co-pilot. "Grab onto something."

From here the computer takes over, calculating the complex set of maneuvers needed to exactly match the derelict ship's speed and direction. You feel the Kestrel shudder through a final series of thrust and counter-thrust micro-adjustments, and then the docking clamps engage with a hollow boom.

Squinting at her hand terminal, Serena's brow furrows. "That's weird..."

"What is?"

"I'm getting no atmospheric reading in certain parts of the ship," she says. "Either they sustained damage, or they dumped most the air."

Serena is cut off by the sharp hiss of hydraulics. The airlock cycles through an array of yellow and green lights, and then the door slides open with a shift of internal pressure. You give your own ship one last reassuring pat and push on through.

The world beyond the airlock is cold and dark. As your eyes adjust, the outline of a room fades into view. Condensation in the form of ice crystals clings to control surfaces and shadowy computer consoles. Everything is in standby mode; all panels are dark except for the red-orange glow of emergency LED's.

The ship is dark, spooky, and deserted.

"I can make my way down to Engineering," Serena suggests. "If I can get the power up we can restart the air scrubbers. Get some atmosphere going in here."

"Probably not a good idea until we know what we're facing," you say, drawing one of your service pistols. "Might be better to stick together until we've secured the ship."

Serena holds up a black box with red and yellow wires protruding from it. "Or I can hook this battery up to the mainframe computer in the Ops room. Make the ship tell us what happened here."

Okay, it's time to choose!

If you want to power up the atmospheric systems, send Serena to Engineering and *TURN TO PAGE 20*

If you'd rather secure the ship first, explore the main corridor and *TURN TO PAGE 35*

If your biggest priority is the ship's mainframe computer, head to Operations and *TURN TO PAGE 81*

You're spilled into a long rectangular room – the biggest you've seen so far. A dozen or more metal tubes line both sides with neat, military precision. Each of them could easily fit a person, with room to spare.

"Well I think we found the crew," Serena tells you. She strides by and steps up to a computer terminal, her fingers beginning their now-familiar dance.

While you wait you examine the tubes. Each is set back on a slight angle, for maximum comfort. Even short voyages across the solar system would take several months, so aside from slowing heartbeat and respiration down to near-hibernetic levels, these chambers were designed to minimize the effects of space travel on the human body.

"Got it," your co-pilot calls out in satisfaction.

The hiss of multiple pressure release valves precedes the simultaneous opening of twenty cylindrical hatches. You squint uneasily through the haze, unsure of what you'll see. The doors open slowly, revealing...

Nothing. Every tube is completely empty.

"What's going on?" Serena exclaims. She thumbs a button and the tubes slowly close. "Where is everyone?"

"An even better question," you ask, "what the heck is this?"

In the center of the room a strange transparent cylinder swirls with silvery white light. The colors dance and whirl behind the glass, chasing each other in a never-ending spiral from floor to ceiling. The cylinder is featureless, except for a small star-shaped depression cut into one side. Above the depression are the letters CTSTASIS

"Cryostasis," you mutter aloud.

"Yeah, maybe. But what's the 'T' for?"

The sudden chime of an alarm grabs your attention. The sound comes from a sloping corridor exiting the room on the left. To the right, a nearly-identical corridor climbs upward in the opposite direction.

If you follow the sound of the alarm, hang and left and *TURN TO PAGE 26*
If you'd rather run up the ramp on your right, *HEAD ON OVER TO PAGE 50*

12

You nod your head in the direction Serena indicated. "Show me what you saw."

The darkness of the left corridor gives way to the dim glow of a standing terminal. Somehow it still has power. Serena punches a few codes on the keypad and the screen erupts with color. Readings and measurements scroll by, giving a full diagnostic of the Dauntless's internal workings.

"The shield emitter is down," you say, scanning the data. "This ship is defenseless."

"Well that's reassuring," Serena quips.

"And look there," you say, pointing. "Most of the turrets are still hot."

Your co-pilot looks uneasy at the news.

"Whatever the Dauntless is," you announce, "it's been in a fight. Recently."

Time's ticking, so you'd better get moving. *TURN TO PAGE 44*

You sprint from the bridge, Serena so close behind you she's practically tripping over your heels. The other ship could be here at any minute. There isn't a lot of time.

In fact, you're moving so fast, you almost miss a legend on the wall. Beneath it, in large letters, the word SECURITY.

"This way!" you call over your shoulder.

Spilling into the next room the two of you catch your breath. The Security deck is neat, clean, orderly. Everything is arranged with military precision, just as you'd expect it to be. Two empty cells are built into the far wall, up against the hull. A rather large weapons locker stands in one corner.

"There."

A minute later you're standing over the locker with a arm's length of steel conduit torn from an electrical cluster. Slowly you raise your arm, taking careful aim at the electromagnetic lock.

"Wait!" Serena cries.

Before you can protest, Serena pulls on the door. The locker swings open easily on well-oiled hinges.

"It's not even locked," she smiles smugly.

Inside the locker are an array of weapons, mostly hand-held. Standing next to them are two rifles. One is long and slender and very familiar. The shorter one is black, and ribbed with strange-looking heat sinks along its length.

"Some security," you tell your co-pilot, hoisting the longer rife. You hand her the shorter one and check the magazine. Both appear loaded.

Serena looks up at you expectantly. "What's next?"

Unmarked exits leave the Security Deck to the left and right.

If you run down the LEFT corridor, *TURN TO PAGE 61*
If you head RIGHT instead, *FLIP OVER TO PAGE 51*

14

The main corridor forks into two smaller hallways, each a mirrored twin of the other. You notice that these, in turn, open into a series of small staterooms.

"The crew's quarters," you announce. "Let's split up. You take that hall, I'll take this one. Search for anything important and meet at the end."

Serena disappears around a corner and you begin going through the rooms. You find each to be a very clean, very neat utilitarian space. There's not much of interest except for a few personal items: a bathrobe here, a pair of reading glasses there. There's no sign of the crew whatsoever.

In one chamber you find a faded photo of a woman in a black and yellow jumpsuit, holding a toddler. In another, a child's drawing of a little girl, roughly labeled 'Emily'. You start feeling guilty for going through other people's stuff. By the time you reach the end, you've found nothing.

Serena rounds the corner where the two corridors come together. She has a strange black rifle slung over her shoulder now. She hands you a longer one, even more sleek and dangerous-looking.

"Thought we could use these," she tells you. "Found them in a weapon's locker."

BOOM!

You don't get a chance to respond as the ship is rocked with a loud, hollow-sounding reverberation. The noise is followed by the unmistakable thump of an electromagnetic seal taking hold.

"Well," you tell your co-pilot. "Looks like they're here."

The party starts when you *TURN TO PAGE 70*

"I can't figure it out either," you say. "We'll have to press a button."

Your co-pilot stares back at you with a gleam in her eye. Serena's always been fierce. Feisty. Defiant. On a whim, you reach down and press the red button.

Nothing happens.

"Well that's not it," you both say at once.

Better pick again.

If you try the BLUE button, *GO TO PAGE 48*
If you'd rather the YELLOW button, *HEAD TO PAGE 77*

16

The room is dim. The lights are flashing. The broken screen is burning your retinas.

You're just about to give up, when all of a sudden something happens... from virtually out of nowhere, the numbers on the monitor solidify and jump out at you!

"Sixteen!" you just about shout. "One Six!"

Serena enters the final part of the sequence code and presses the ENTER button. There's an visual alarm followed by the loud droning of a klaxon horn. Every console in the room erupts with light.

"CODE ACCEPTED," a feminine computerized voice calls from overhead. "EJECTION SEQUENCE INITIATED."

"That did it!" Serena cries.

"Yeah?"

"Yes," your co-pilot says, leaping to her feet. Somewhere in the decks beneath you, a series of very strange whooshing and humming sounds has started up. You'd swear you felt the floor shift, too.

"SECONDARY COMMAND CODE CHANGED. NEW COMMAND CODE IS SET TO ONE-FOUR-ZERO."

"What's that?" you ask. "One four zero?"

Serena shrugs. She grabs your hand.

"Out of here?" you ask.

"Totally."

A plasma injection assembly dump sounds like a good thing *not* to be around for, doesn't it?

Which is why you should *HEAD TO PAGE 115*

"Ship Alexa this is Lt. Colonel Andon Mercer of the EWC Kestrel," you say into the mic. "We DO require assistance. Do you copy? We DO require–"

A response comes faintly through amidst the static. It's impossible to make it out.

"Alexa, we have been cut off from our ship by an armed vessel of unknown origin. Please proceed with caution. I repeat, we DO require assistance..."

The channel explodes with feedback and then abruptly goes silent. You look at Serena. "Did they hear us?"

She shrugs. "Maybe." Your co-pilot switches the overhead monitor to a split-screen of external cameras. "All we can do now is wait."

It doesn't take long for the Alexa to match the Dauntless's trajectory. As it approaches on a standard vector, you realize the ship is a lot smaller than you thought. You hadn't taken that into consideration when asking for help.

Suddenly there's movement on the other side of the screen. You can only watch, powerless to do anything, as the jagged enemy mothership begins engaging the new vessel. There's a brief, brilliant battle, and then the Alexa floats off in three separate, distinct pieces.

"Did we just–"

"Yeah," you say defeatedly. A sick feeling steals over you. "I think we did."

When the Blackthorne arrives you'll have a lot of explaining to do. The EWC will have to do even more explaining to the Mars-Jupiter Alliance regarding their missing ship. Hopefully you haven't started an intra-system war. That is, if you ever get back in one piece to worry about such things.

Whether or not you get off the Dauntless alive, it looks like this is

THE END

18

You enter the Hazardous Cargo deck, a smaller version of the Dauntless's main cargo bay. This one is devoid of pretty much everything. A tremendous piece of retractable titanium stretches across one wall, the first of two doors that make up the waste processing airlock. Two large containers of spent fuel rods are marked with a biohazard symbol, while a large, anti-gravity handtruck hovers beside a computer terminal, ready for use.

"We've come in a circle," Serena says. She points to an exit on the opposite side. "We're almost back to–"

The rest of the words die in her throat. On the far side of the high chamber, a pair of the creatures drag themselves in. Silently you watch as they stretch to their full, terrifying height. Then one of them sees you. It screams in what could possibly be triumph.

"Quick," Serena cries, "the lift!" From the corner of your eye, you see that the cargo lift doors are still open.

You point to the opposite exit. "But don't we need to go that way?"

"Yes, but... them!"

Hurriedly you glance down at the AG-handtruck. It's massive – even bigger than them. An idea forms in your head, but it's risky. The creatures are charging... there's no time!

If you jump into the safety of the cargo lift, *FLIP TO PAGE 86*

If you decide to use the anti-gravity handtruck, roll a single die (or just choose a random number from 1 to 6)

If the number comes up a 1 or 2, *GO TO PAGE 88*

If the number ends up as a 3, 4, 5 or 6, *HEAD TO PAGE 137*

"You're right of course," you tell Serena. "Let's get to the Kestrel."

You glance down one last time at the shimmering star-shaped chunk of glass. A nagging feeling tugs at the back of your mind. Wasn't there something more to it? You guess it doesn't matter now. You drop it and run.

Thankfully, the corridors between you and the Kestrel are empty. The ship is unharmed, untouched. Together you and Serena seal the airlock behind you, disengage the docking clamps, and begin prepping the ship for departure.

You don't feel safe until the Dauntless is a grey, baseball-sized blur out the port-side window. Glancing back, you're still troubled by the ship itself. What was it there for? Where was its crew? You ponder these questions in silence for a while, until your viewport fills with an enormous behemoth of a war vessel; the Blackthorne.

"And you destroyed this 'alien' ship all by yourself?" Commodore Garriott asks. You docked with the Blackthorne less than an hour ago. Your debriefing was immediate.

"My co-pilot did, yes," you answer. "She accessed the other vessel remotely and overloaded its core."

"From the..." he pauses to glance at his screen. "The Dauntless, you say?"

"Yes sir." You glance over at Serena. "Of course, you'll find all this on the ship's computer. The Dauntless, I mean."

The man's expression is impossible to read. His face is granite. He glances out through the viewport, where the Dauntless floats idle. Two of the Blackthorne's own boarding parties are already hard at work securing the ship.

"Yes," he continues. "Yes, well fine job." He scratches his beard. "Excellent work, actually." You know coming from him, the praise really means something. The Commodore is the hardest man to please in the entire fleet.

"Get some rest and report back here tomorrow, *Colonel*. From there we'll talk about your next assignment."

Great job! You saved the Dauntless, the Kestrel, and even the solar system! I'd say you should be more than happy. For right now at least, this is

THE END

20

"Getting the air going is crucial," you tell Serena. "Maybe you should get to Engineering and do your thing. I'll stick around here and see what else I can find."

Your co-pilot nods as she activates her wrist-light. Flashing the beam before her, she ducks through one of the exits.

The room seems even darker with Serena gone. You move around slowly, examining things with the beam from your own light. Everything seems ghostly. Forgotten. There are no signs of life.

Eventually you notice a dim glow emanating somewhere off to your right. A closer inspection reveals a side corridor, brighter than the others. You also detect faint sounds coming from that direction.

You've got a decision to make here.

If you'd like to explore the dim corridor, gather your courage and *TURN TO PAGE 138*

If you think Serena might need some, ummm, help (or something), follow her back to engineering and *GO TO PAGE 91*

"See if you can bypass the system," you tell your co-pilot. "Smashing this thing might do even more damage to the internals than you'd ever do with that computer terminal."

Serena laughs mischievously. "Then you don't know the damage I can do with this computer terminal."

Once again she goes to work. Her fingers are a blur on the keypad – they move so fast you can barely even follow them. You find yourself wondering where she learned to type like that.

"That one," she says, pointing to one of the long metal cylinders. "Almost got it... I think."

You both turn to look expectantly at the stasis tube.

Did she do it? Roll one die (or just think of a random number from 1 to 6)
If the number is a 1, 3 or 5, *TURN TO PAGE 22*
If the number is a 2, 4, or 6, *TURN TO PAGE 92*

22

You wait and you wait...

And then you wait.

A minute crawls by, and absolutely nothing happens.

"Smash it?" you ask finally. Serena just shrugs and nods.

Make your best fist and *TURN TO PAGE 82*

You run. A set of ramps takes you into the lower decks, where everything is more open and less finished. You pass bulkheads and structural supports. Massive struts poured of steel thicker than your arm.

Up ahead, the hum of machinery seems exceptionally loud and obnoxious. Maybe you can lose your pursuers there, amongst the noise.

Four enormous tanks make up the Dauntless's water purification and storage systems. In and around the massive cisterns the space is filled with filter arrays and irradiation systems designed to reclaim every last drop of moisture that comes down here.

"Let's hide," Serena suggests. She literally has to shout to be heard. "Maybe they'll run past us."

You frown. By now you're getting tired of running and hiding. Perhaps it's time for something different.

Serena's right. Usually. If you go with her idea, play hide and seek by *TURNING TO PAGE 49*

Then again, maybe it's time to make a stand. If so, *FLIP AHEAD TO PAGE 75*

24

You decide the lifeboat is a dead end. If the monster cornered you in there you'd be trapped!

An inhuman scream tells you you've been spotted. Thinking fast you point to a bulky stack of containers on one side of the hallway. Drawing your weapons, both you and Serena begin firing at the base of the tower. The bottom container disintegrates, causing the stack to topple over and block most of the corridor.

"I'm getting tired of running," you tell her as you flee in the opposite direction.

"Me too," Serena agrees. "Let's work our way back to the Kestrel."

Keep it moving. *TURN TO PAGE 54*

"Let's play it safe. I'm going to launch one and one."

Serena acknowledges your decision as the firing solution is re-verified. You prep tubes one and three, wait for the board to go green, then press the launch button.

On screen, the two torpedoes take very different trajectories. One – the high-explosive shell – heads straight for its target. The heat-seeker however doesn't do anything. It veers off in the opposite direction, refusing to find anything to lock onto.

Eagerly you watch the first projectile. The enemy ship doesn't move, doesn't flinch. It's going to hit! But at the very last moment, the torpedo explodes. A pair of sickly green beams emanate from the other ship's bow, shooting the torpedo down before it can reach its target.

"So close," Serena laments.

As you continue watching, the alien ship shifts position. What looks to be its nose is now pointed in your direction. The two circular ports on the bow still glow green. They might even be gaining in brightness...

"C'mon!" you shout, pulling your co-pilot through the nearest exit. "We're out of here!"

RUN AHEAD TO PAGE 63

26

You head down a series of ramps, the blare of the alarm growing ever louder as you approach a large, well-lit area. You'd recognize it immediately as the Engineering Deck, even if not for the pair of mammoth casings that house the Dauntless's twin beamed-thermal engines.

"Something's wrong!" Serena yells. She's shouting over the sound of the alarm, but also over the noise of the engines. You're no better than an amateur mechanic, but you can tell right away it's way louder than it should be.

A terminal on the wall gives you the rough details; damage control reports indicate the rear of the ship has been shot to pieces. The starboard engine has taken heavy damage as well, and the temperature has already climbed past dangerous levels.

"They've red-lined it," you tell Serena. "Whoever they are, the ship's throttle is pinned."

Your co-pilot checks the readouts and nods her agreement. The room itself is searingly hot. Your hair is plastered to your forehead. Serena is also sweating.

"Is it dangerous?" you ask.

"Not yet," she replies. "But I wouldn't want to stay here for too long."

Along the starboard casing you notice several coolant leaks that are affecting the engine's temperature. If you could close some of those valves, the existing cooling systems would become that much more effective.

The only problem: you're too large to fit in the gap between the casing and the wall. You could send Serena in though, and try and talk her through it.

If you think you can talk Serena through fixing the leaks, *SKIP DOWN TO PAGE 68*

If you'd rather just get out of Engineering altogether, *FLIP OVER TO PAGE 36*

"Look out!"

The explosion happens without warning. Having detected your signal, the enemy ship pinpoints the external Auxiliary Comm array and opens fire.

The last thing you see is a bright green light. Very, very bright.

Hey, at least it was quick. But this is definitely

THE END

28

The power core paints the room a glowing, ghastly blue. The console beckons you...

"This isn't a bad idea," you tell your co-pilot, "but maybe you're right. Let's leave it alone for now."

Serena sighs heavily, appearing totally relieved by your decision. Even more so when you take your hands away from the controls.

"We can always come back here," you say. "But first, let's find a clear path to the Kestrel." An ominous thought suddenly occurs to you. "If those things haven't found her already."

That exact thought does wonders for quickening your pace.

Follow Serena out of the Reactor Room and *TURN TO PAGE 18*

The monster is too close to the exposed hull. If you missed with the rifle you could punch a hole straight through it, and the resulting decompression would mean Adios Muchachos.

You pull out of your service pistols instead. At the very least, maybe you could distract it long enough to keep it away from your co-pilot.

You fire a few shots that bounce harmlessly off the creature's armor. Your tactic works all too well – it whirls back to face you. But then, before it can charge, the room fills with a horrendous crash. Serena has picked up the pipe and used it to knock out the legs of a very tall rack overloaded with heavy engine parts. Several tons of metal and debris spill between you, bisecting the room with junk.

"Here!" yells Serena, pulling you into another corridor. There's no time to look back. The monster is already crashing through the pile...

FLIP BACK TO PAGE 23

30

You eye the robot's faceplate, looking for the button or switch that will power it down. You think you have it picked out when it lunges at you with the power drill.

"Hey!" Serena cries loudly. "Over here!"

Her attempts at gaining the robot's attention fail miserably. Luckily you're able to dodge the drill, which drives a deadly-looking hole right into the cargo container directly behind you.

Quickly you reach out and flip the large blue switch. Rather than turn the robot off, the flames of the plasma welder flare even more brightly!

Again the loadbot rushes you. Again you duck. This time the drill clangs off your helmet before embedding itself in another container. Your hand goes up to search for a hole, but thankfully one isn't there.

CRASH!

Nearby, a stack of four empty containers suddenly falls over. In response, the loadbot's head whirls around. It stops, pivots, and speeds toward the fallen crates.

The robot is almost finished re-stacking them when Serena knocks over another tower, this one even taller than the first. The bot zips over to that stack as well, deftly grabbing each container and setting it down on the previous one.

"Nice work!" you say, getting back to your feet. "What made you–"

Serena doesn't answer. Grabbing your hand, your co-pilot pulls you in the direction of a side exit. On the way out, she stops to kick over one last stack for good measure.

Looks like you definitely owe her one.

Now *TURN TO PAGE 66*

You keep firing, hypnotized by the silent recoil of the massive quad barrels. The cannon is a living thing, surging beneath you. You watch with anticipation as shots streak toward the enemy, and then your HUD flashes white and yellow with a perfect target lock.

You hit it!

Bolts of plasma explode against the hull of the boarding ship, shredding what looks to be some kind of communications array on its starboard side. Debris floats everywhere. The ship begins venting something white and milky into space, but then the engines kick in and it passes beyond the scope of your target arc.

"That was nice," Serena says admiringly. "I didn't know you could–"

The Dauntless is rocked by a sudden explosion. Something flashes on your console, and you can see that one of the other PDC's just blinked out of existence. The other ship was hit, but not disabled. It's still coming.

"They're taking out the turrets!" you shout, leaping from the chair. Serena is still hunched over a terminal when you pull her through the doorway. Just in time too, because the PDC station explodes behind you in a burst of blinding green light...

Quick! *TURN TO PAGE 57*

32

Inaction really doesn't sit well with you. Never has.

You rush forward through the darkness, in the direction you last remember seeing Serena. You're stopped quickly as a hand clamps itself over your mouth. Serena whispers a "shhh..." in one ear and you go totally silent, listening for any sounds of whatever else came into the room. Again you hear a growl. Again, it's close.

The room explodes with brightness as Serena's wrist-lamp flicks on. You see a giant red eye segmented into four distinct yellow pupils... pupils that dilate almost to nothing as your co-pilot flashes her lamp straight into a creature's face.

Its arms go up to protect itself. Instinctively, you kick it square in the chest. Your foot bounces off one of the strange metal plates, but the momentum is enough to send the thing sprawling backward with a crash and a loud thud.

The auxiliary lighting kicks in. Your opponent is sprawled over the splintered remains of a small couch. You move to kick it again, but Serena is pulling you sideways. Together you duck through a service door and begin flying down a series of metal steps.

Head down, down, down by *TURNING TO PAGE 64*

There's no way to fight the monster. And even if there was, there's just no time.

You bolt after Serena. There's no time to look back. You can't think, you can't reason... your brain is consumed with the process of making your legs move as fast as they can. Faster than ever before, in your entire life.

"The Kestrel should be this way," Serena pants when you finally catch up. "We're not far from–"

Her sentence dies. You look up again, and then you see why.

Three of the creatures block the corridor ahead of you. There are no other exits. No alcoves or access hatches or air ducts. Nothing to get you out of this. Not this time.

And in the back of your mind, the countdown. The reactor, spinning itself purple. The heat of the power core steadily rising. Unfixable, unrecoverable...

You got far. Really far. But at this point, unfortunately, this is going to be

THE END

34

The invaders are too big, and there are too many of them for a firefight. Fresh out of ideas you turn your attention downward, to your newfound grenades.

The high-explosive might work, but you're too close to the Dauntless's hull to risk it. Motioning Serena behind you, you pull the pin on a pair of concussion grenades and roll them in the direction of your new friends.

BOOM! BOOM!

The explosion clears the hall, blowing both you and the creatures in opposite directions. You and your co-pilot skid to a halt and scramble quickly to your feet. Serena is shouting something but you can't tell what it is; you're totally deaf – at least for now – and your head feels like you just got kicked in both ears.

Smoke and debris threaten to cut you off from each other. Pulling Serena close you happen to look up and notice the concussion has blown open a large vent from the overhead ductwork. You point, Serena nods, and then you're lifting her up and into the air duct.

Seconds later you're pulling the vent closed behind you and crawling down a series of narrow but well-hidden ventilation tubes. They could go anywhere, really, but you're happy with that as long as anywhere is not here.

Good job getting out of there. *TURN TO PAGE 123*

"Let's stick together for now," you say. "When we're confident the ship is secure we can start trying to figure out what happened."

Your co-pilot nods and together you advance into the Dauntless's wide central corridor. Darkness blankets the ship. Everything is cold and frosty as you use your wrist-lamps to pick through the shadows.

"WHOA!"

A loud clang rings out suddenly from behind. In a single motion you whirl, crouch down, and aim your service pistol at the source of the noise.

Just as quickly, Serena's hand goes over your own.

"Easy," she tells you. "We need to keep our heads screwed on straight."

A long slow breath forces you to relax. You can see now that Serena accidentally kicked over the plate from an open hatch, nothing more.

Continuing on, a cluster of rooms on one side of the corridor turn out to be utility closets. Everything is neat, orderly. There's no sign of anyone. The darkness is broken only by the occasional blink of tiny but colorful auxiliary lights.

"I think I see something with power," Serena says all of a sudden.

Up ahead the corridor makes a 'T'. Serena is pointing to the left. To the right, the corridor seems to end in an enormous, yawning chamber.

If you head toward the source of Serena's hunch, *FLIP OVER TO PAGE 12*

If you think the big room seems more interesting, *CHECK IT OUT ON PAGE 44*

36

Another series of corridors brings you to a wide, unlocked door. You thumb the open button, and enter the Dauntless's Bridge.

"Now we're talking," Serena says approvingly. She picks out the master control station and gets to work on the computer.

In the meantime you circle the bridge, marveling at its construction. The room is an elongated oval. The walls are of some polished white material, reinforced with curved supports that look both futuristic and ancient at the same time. Some of the panels actually have detail. They remind you of a series of Art Deco paintings you once saw in a museum.

The bridge isn't perfect however. Some of it has sustained damage. A row of blown panels line the left-hand wall, and at some point there looks to have been a fire up near the ceiling. Debris litters the floor. You kick a few chunks of hardened sealing foam and drag your foot through powder from what might've been a fire extinguisher.

A scene suddenly blinks on the main viewscreen. You recognize it as the bridge, but now it's filled with about eight or ten people dressed in black and yellow jumpsuits.

"This is the last recording," Serena tells you. "Actually, it's the only recording."

She hits the PLAY button.

Movie time.

There's no sound on the screen as the scene plays out. The men and women in jumpsuits move about frantically, working the controls. Whatever they're to accomplish, they can't seem to do it fast enough. There's a sense of urgency... and foreboding.

Without warning the ship is rocked by an explosion. Damage begins to appear. It matches the damage you've already seen all around you.

"Why can't we hear what they're saying?"

Serena shakes her head but doesn't answer. She points back to the recording. On the other crew's screen you can see something chasing the Dauntless. It's another ship. It looks very large and unusually shaped. Sort of like a sickle.

As you continue to watch the other bridge begins filling with smoke. Finally the screen goes dark, and there's nothing else. You stare over at the captain's chair. It stands sentinel in the center of the room, empty and abandoned.

"What happened to–"

Your co-pilot presses another series of buttons. Directly above you the armored shield retracts from the massive, 360-degree viewport. Through the glass, the enemy ship comes into view. Curved. Menacing. Filled with spikes.

And a *lot* closer than it was in the recording.

"That ship's not..."

"Human?" you finish for Serena. "No. It sure isn't."

Outside, beyond the viewport, you pick up signs of motion. Another, smaller ship detaches from the larger one. It accelerates away from the mother vessel, then turns in a wide arc as it heads unmistakably in your direction.

An array of lights begins blinking wildly across the bridge's main console. Simultaneously, an alarm goes off somewhere behind you.

"Well," you tell your co-pilot. "I guess we have some friends are coming over."

Looks like things are heating up! *TURN TO PAGE 13*

38

You DUCK! And just in time, too...

A thick metal arm swings past your head with a loud whoosh. You sidestep, recover, and spin around to face it.

"It's a loadbot!" Serena cries. The machine whirs and clicks as it moves toward you. Despite its bulk, you know the huge robot is programmed with unnerving precision and agility.

"Hey," you tell the bot. "I'm not trying to–"

Your sentence is cut off as the machine rushes you in a burst of speed. Its loading arms are empty, but it could easily use them to impale you against one of the many shipping containers.

"What the heck does it want?" Serena cries.

You bite back a sarcastic remark. "I don't know, why don't you ask it!"

Your co-pilot opens her mouth as if to do just that when the mech rushes again. This time it brings the pincer-like claws of its secondary arms around. In one 'hand' it clutches a rapidly-spinning power drill. In the other, you see the blue-white sparks of a 9000°F plasma welder.

The loadbot is still coming. You'd better think fast...

You notice the bot has a series of controls surrounding its face-plate.

If you think you're fast enough to power it down, give your reflexes a shot and *TURN TO PAGE 30*

If you think it's time to finally use that pistol, aim very carefully before *FLIPPING TO PAGE 104*

If you'd rather just duck and run, *FLEE QUICKLY TO PAGE 90*

40

"Step back," you tell Serena.

She moves clear as you jump into the turret. Your hands close comfortably around the sticks, your boots snapping into the swivel pedals as the cannon slides comfortably beneath you.

The heads-up display materializes in your line of vision. Your eyes scroll through speed and trajectory readouts for both ships, ammo counts, firing solutions...

THWAP! THWAP! THWAP! THWAP!

You waste no time. The four barrels of your point defense cannon fire 1/10th of a second behind each other in a rapid, never-ending circle. Bright red bolts of superheated plasma streak through the darkness, arcing out toward your target.

Did you hit it? Roll one die (or just think of a random number from 1 to 6)

If the number is a 1, 2, or 3, *GO TO PAGE 84*

If the number is a 4 or 5, *TURN TO PAGE 31*

If the number is a 6, *HEAD ON OVER TO PAGE 122*

"Step aside for a second," you tell Serena. She looks back at you curiously as she makes room. A few keystrokes later, you've achieved victory. The screen unlocks and fills with information, top to bottom.

"You did it!" Serena practically screams. "How–"

"Later," you tell her. You point back to the terminal. "Right now, do your thing."

Things get serious as Serena turns her full attention to what she's doing. The strange liquid screen scrolls by with so much information your head starts to hurt. For once, none of the creatures show up to crash the party. You guess their own ship might be the last place they'd look.

"Okay, this is their power core," Serena says, pointing. A smirk crosses her face. "You're not going to believe this, but I can totally access it."

"Good, then do it." She nods. You don't even have to tell her what 'it' is. A minute later, all of the lights on the boarding vessel start flashing. On screen, the mothership's lights start doing the same. Serena points out heat and power readouts that climb rapidly. Already most of them are in the red.

"Can they stop it?"

Your co-pilot shakes her head solemnly. "Probably not. Their ship has an internal brain, more so than a computer," she explains. "After I super-charged the core, I short-circuited the whole thing on the way out."

As you watch, the sickle-shaped ship begins a slow rotation. It flashes yellow, then green, then goes almost black in color. The vessel fires its engines in an attempt to limp away from the Dauntless, and then all of a sudden the acceleration stops. Dozens of tiny ships, even smaller than the landing vessel you're on, rocket away from the mothership in every possible direction. Engines screaming, they flee into the void.

"It's gonna–"

Your sentence is finished by a silent, brilliant explosion. The Dauntless is bathed for a moment in a pallid green light, and when you look again all that remains of the other ship is glittering space-dust.

42

Serena is still gaping at the viewscreen when you drag her back to reality.

"Come on," you tell her. "Those things are still on this ship, and they're not going to be happy with us. Now more than ever, we've got to get back to the Kestrel."

You step into the corridor and get your bearings. Your ship isn't far. If you could only avoid running into the creatures one last time, you can make your way to the airlock and be off the Dauntless before they even realize it.

You're almost out of the hall when your foot hits something solid. You look down and see a strange, shimmering piece of glass. It's glowing faintly...

And it's in the shape of a star.

"Wait! I know what this is!"

"What?" Serena calls back. She's already ten steps ahead of you.

"Well, I might not know what it is... but I know *where* it goes!"

"Andon, we don't have time! The Kestrel, remember?"

If you know where the strange star-shaped disc goes, use the chart below to add up all the letters in the word that was written above it. When you have the total you can *GO TO THAT PAGE*

A = 1	F = 6	K = 11	P = 16	U = 21	Z = 26
B = 2	G = 7	L = 12	Q = 17	V = 22	Example:
C = 3	H = 8	M = 13	R = 18	W = 23	ANNA =
D = 4	I = 9	N = 14	S = 19	X = 24	1+14+14+1
E = 5	J = 10	O = 15	T = 20	Y = 25	= 30

If you think maybe Serena is right, and it really is time to leave the Dauntless, sprint back to your ship and *TURN TO PAGE 19*

You freeze, totally and completely. Standing silent with ears open, you let the darkness amplify all sound.

Behind you, you can still hear something moving. It's getting closer now, almost to within striking distance. Whatever it is, it sounds heavy. It makes a low rustling sound against the floor, with an occasional metallic scraping.

When you feel the first faint traces of hot breath on your neck, you act. Whipping around, you smash the thing full in the face with the butt of your rifle. There's the loud, wet snap of cartilage or bone – or maybe both – and then all of a sudden the auxiliary lights blink on.

You find yourself standing over one of the creatures. Its face is a mess of... well, you really can't tell. You must've knocked it out cold though, because it's not even moving. It is still breathing however, as evidenced by the slow rise and fall of its massive chest.

"How hard did you hit that thin–"

Serena's question is cut off as the Turbo Lift abruptly begins descending beside you. Someone is calling it from the lower floor. Or more accurately, some *thing*.

You point out a service stairwell and quickly push the door open. "The Kestrel," you tell your co-pilot as you wave her through. "Right now it's all that matters."

Head back down? Why not! *FLIP TO PAGE 64*

44

The corridor ends at the Dauntless's Cargo Deck – an enormous loading area that takes up an entire corner of the ship. The first thing you notice is that gravity exists here. Although the ship's systems are still unrestored, it's obvious that an emergency backup must power the zone. The hold itself is more than three-quarters full. Crates and containers lay stacked in neat rows along most of the floor. In some places they even stretch from floor to ceiling.

"At least we can find out what this ship is carrying," you tell Serena. You unseal the clips of the nearest container and pop it open, only to find it empty.

Box after box, there's nothing in any of the crates. Together you try different sizes, different rows, but no matter which containers you open, the results are always the same.

"Who lugs around an entire hold full of empty containers?" you ask. "What kind of ship is this?"

"Maybe the containers *are* the cargo!" Serena laughs. You'd thump her on the head, if not for her helmet.

Abruptly, Serena's gaze moves to a point over your shoulder. Her eyes go wide.

"Andon!"

If you duck, *GO TO PAGE 38*
If you don't, just close the book and pretend you're unconscious.

"Hang on," Serena cries. "I almost have it! I almost have–"

"LOCKDOWN. LOCKDOWN. LOCKDOWN."

There's the hiss of hydraulics as a second pair of shield doors slam shut over the normal ones. Constructed of two-inch thick layered steel, they erase any last hope of breaking your way out.

"SECONDARY COMMAND ISOLATED. SECURITY TEAMS HAVE BEEN NOTIFIED."

You shoulders slump. Serena is face-down on her console, both hands clutching her head in frustration.

"So close..." she groans.

Above you, one of the many screens begins to blink. You recognize the sound of a proximity alarm, alerting you to the presence of an incoming ship.

"Maybe it's the Blackthorne," you offer hopefully.

Serena eventually raises her head to stare at the screen. She looks utterly defeated.

Maybe you're about to get rescued. Or maybe something more sinister is about to happen. Either way, at least you won't spend the rest of your life in lockdown, waiting for a security team that's never going to arrive.

Unfortunately however, your adventure on the Dauntless has reached

---

THE END

46

"Stand back for a minute," you tell Serena.

She moves off to the side of the medical cabinet as you step forward and place your hand on the latch. You lock eyes with her, then silently count together:

ONE... TWO...

On 'three' you fling open the door and take a giant step back. Inside is... nobody.

"Nothing but sheets and pillowcases," you tell her. "What give–"

Suddenly something flies out of the metal locker. Serena's scream is so loud and piercing it turns all the blood in your veins to ice. You're pretty sure something terrible just happened... until she smiles, reaches down, and picks up a gigantic grey cat.

"Awww..."

Your whole body shakes with adrenaline. As you check to see if you've jumped out of your skin, Serena checks a blue metal tag around the cat's neck.

"King!" she declares. Gingerly she begins stroking the cat's thick fur. "Hey boy... hey King... where is everybody?"

The cat answers her by leaping out of your co-pilot's arms. It darts out of the room, turns the corner, and disappears.

"He's as friendly as everything else in this place," you quip. "Come on. We need to keep going."

Well, at least you found *someone!* *NOW TURN TO PAGE 14*

48

"I still can't see it," you say. "What do we do now?"

Serena points to the three colorful flashing buttons. "One of them will do an emergency dump of the injection assembly. But we don't know which."

You look down quickly and make a snap decision. "Blue."

Serena hits the button...

Instantly the room – no the entire ship – begins vibrating at impossibly high speeds. Your hands slam over your ears to escape the noise. Your teeth begin clacking together so hard, you're afraid they'll shatter.

"The magnetic field generator!" Serena shouts. "We turned it *on!*"

Overloaded with record levels of scalding hot plasma, the shield emitter flies violently apart. So does the room. So does the upper part of the ship.

The blue button was very pretty. But pressing it means this is

THE END

Serena points to a gap between two of the tanks. Squeezing through, you find yourselves in a small triangular area with little room to maneuver. You press as flat as you can, with your backs to the hull.

"I don't like this," you tell Serena. "If they find us here, we're–"

An enormous crash is followed by a series of grunts and deep guttural noises. Together you freeze, both you and your co-pilot trying your best to stay utterly motionless...

Grab a coin and flip it until it hits the ceiling. Let it land without catching it.

If it comes up heads, *TURN TO PAGE 97*

If it comes up tails, *FLIP AHEAD TO PAGE 72*

50

The series of ramps eventually levels out, exiting into a wide corridor fed by a handful of smaller ones. Going with the flow, you and Serena find yourselves beneath the lights of a brightly-lit Mess Hall.

An array of chairs are bolted to the floor beneath two smooth white tables. Along the walls you see banks of food dispensers, convection ovens, and sanitizing stations. Everything is pristine, immaculate. The air smells vaguely of lemons. Whoever is responsible for keeping this place is doing a fine job.

"What, no coffee?" Serena asks. Her hands move over the consoles, trying to find anything resembling a java-machine. Her search comes up empty.

"We could try the kitchen," you say, pointing to the obvious archway. A coffee break wasn't part of the Commodore's orders, but then again he didn't say you *couldn't* take one.

If you continue the Quest for Coffee, enter the kitchen and *FLIP TO PAGE 83*
Otherwise just keep moving and *TURN TO PAGE 36*

You follow a curved passage along the hull of the ship. Before you, the passage continues. Off to the side stands the convex curvature of the starboard airlock. It looks cold and empty.

"Maybe the crew left through here?" your co-pilot offers. She approaches the door, looking for anything significant. "One way... or another?"

The very thought sends shivers straight through you. Then again, you haven't found any sign of a single soul on board. It's like the entire crew of the Dauntless just up and disappeared.

Suddenly the hiss of hydraulics fills the room. The pressure doors slam shut at double-speed, separating you from Serena. She's sealed inside the airlock! There's a hollow boom as the locking mechanism kicks in.

"UNAUTHORIZED PERSONNEL DETECTED," a voice rumbles from above. You look around in every direction, thoroughly confused.

"AIRLOCK WILL BE AUTO-PURGED IN 10 SECONDS..."

Serena screams, but you can't even hear her. You watch in horror as she runs up to the viewing window and begins pounding frantically on the glass.

52

You scramble around for the override! All you can find is the control terminal. You'll need to log in quickly if you want to stop the countdown and keep the outer doors from flushing the contents of the airlock – and your co-pilot – out into the cold void of space.

"SEVEN SECONDS..." the voice announces. "SIX SECONDS..."

"Serena, what do I do?" you scream, already knowing she can't hear you. "The bypass code! What was it?"

"FIVE SECONDS..."

Serena is shouting a single word but you can't make it out. Then she makes two elongated circles with her hands and holds them side by side.

"FOUR SECONDS... THREE SECONDS..."

The symbol reminds you of something.

"TWO SECONDS..."

If you know the bypass code, use the chart below to add up all the letters in the word. When you have the total you can *GO TO THAT PAGE*

A = 1	F = 6	K = 11	P = 16	U = 21	Z = 26
B = 2	G = 7	L = 12	Q = 17	V = 22	Example:
C = 3	H = 8	M = 13	R = 18	W = 23	ANNA =
D = 4	I = 9	N = 14	S = 19	X = 24	1+14+14+1
E = 5	J = 10	O = 15	T = 20	Y = 25	= 30

If you don't remember the bypass code, or can't figure it out, *TURN TO PAGE 139*

The center corridor narrows out, leading toward the rear of the ship. Suddenly something familiar catches your eye. You stop abruptly and slide open a thick, curved door, revealing a firing station for the aft Point Defense Cannons.

Serena is halfway down the next hall when you pull her back. "Wait! I can operate this turret manually!"

"Really?"

"Oh yeah," you say with confidence. You point past the turret's quad barrels and out through the viewport. The boarding vessel is getting closer. Already it's in range.

"Maybe we could hail them," Serena offers. She begins searching the controls for a radio transmitter. "See what they actually want."

"Or maybe I should blow them to dust and shrapnel before they get here," you counter. "These are the guys the Dauntless was running from. Remember?"

If you're itching to fire those Point Defense Cannons, *TURN TO PAGE 40*
Otherwise, give Serena the opportunity to hail them by *FLIPPING TO PAGE 62*

54

You enter a small area used as an Auxiliary Communications station. A bank of monitoring screens displays video feeds from various parts of the ship. On some of them, you can see the hulking forms of the invaders, moving systematically as they search – presumably for you – room by room, corridor by corridor.

"Look at the size of them," Serena breathes.

"If they reach the Kestrel we have no way home," you remind her. "So let's figure this out."

Using the monitors, you try to determine which corridors will take you back to your own ship. Serena flips through feeds from all different decks. There's still no sign of the Dauntless's crew. All you can see are the creatures, making their way along.

"What do you think they want?" you wonder aloud.

"Don't know." Serena hesitates, then picks at a few buttons on the console. An image of the creatures' larger ship – the mothership – appears on screen. "Want me to ask them?"

You pause for a moment, then shrug. "I guess you can try. But we don't even know what frequency they'd pick up on."

If you know the frequency the Dauntless was already tuned in to, *TURN TO THAT PAGE NUMBER*

If not, you can still try to wing it. In that case *GO TO PAGE 108*

You thumb the activation sequence for the heat-seekers. At this range you can't miss. You double-check your target lock, then fire...

There's a rumble beneath you as the torpedoes leave their tubes. They track outward...

"They're not turning," Serena says flatly.

Your heart sinks in disappointment. The torpedoes don't acquire their target at all. It's like the enemy ship is masking its heat signature. Or perhaps it doesn't even have one.

"Andon..."

The tension in Serena's voice pulls your attention back to the screen, where the enemy ship has launched a salvo of its own. Two deadly-looking green beams slice through the void. With unerring accuracy, they slam into the torpedo bay directly beneath you.

There's a horrific explosion, and then the floor begins disintegrating. It tilts forward and you're slipping, falling... unable to prevent the fact that this is

THE END

56

"We've been running in circles," you tell Serena. "Who's to say if we'll ever get back here? This might be our only chance to do this."

Your co-pilot pauses to consider the gravity of the situation. She nods gravely. "Okay. How can I help?"

Together you go over the sequence of events needed to place the Dauntless in an unrecoverable overload. Serena provides the access codes. You re-route the cooling systems so that the temperature of the power core will rise incrementally. In just a few minutes, everything is ready. Your hand hovers over the 'execute' button.

"Run it," Serena says firmly.

You punch the screen, and the reactor fluctuates in color. It will continuing growing a deeper and deeper blue, eventually reaching a beautiful violet color before melting its way through the floor and then the hull. By then you expect to be on the Kestrel, thousands of kilometers away. Or so you hope.

A loud grunt brings you spinning around. While you were preoccupied, one of the creatures made its way inside! It glances from you, to the core, and back again. Then it begins sprinting at you with surprising, terrifying speed.

"Through here!" Serena cries. She's pointing to one of the four main exits. "Hurry!"

The creature is thundering down the catwalk on all fours. You've got a half-second to decide what to do.

If you run after Serena as fast as you can, *TURN TO PAGE 33*

Or maybe this time you've got another idea. If so, *TURN TO PAGE 116*

You half-run, half-trip into the hallway beyond the PDC Station. You sprawl helplessly to the floor, but thankfully, Serena's arm goes up and slams the emergency button for the pressure doors.

Just in time, the doors seal shut. Beyond a thin glass viewport on either side, you both watch as the entire PDC assembly is torn free of the Dauntless. The twisted metal dome cartwheels wildly, flung into the void in the aftermath of explosive decompression.

"Wow."

Your thoughts echo Serena's sentiment exactly. Other than that, there's not much else to say.

You both catch your breath for a minute before rising to your feet again.

"Let's go. They'll be here soon... and now they're gonna be *really* mad."

TURN TO PAGE 132

58

"UNAUTHORIZED ACCESS ATTEMPTED." The computer's voice is unnervingly calm. "LOCKDOWN IMMINENT."

"Serena!"

"LOCKDOW–"

The overhead voice stops mid-sentence.

"YES!" Serena cries victoriously. In a dizzying blur of light and motion, all the consoles around you spring to life. There's a distinct *THUNK* as the electromagnetic doors unseal themselves. Everything, you realize, is now firmly under your partner's control.

"Who's the master?" Serena yells, throwing her arms into the air. "Who's the mast–"

You co-pilot jumps up so quickly she actually falls out of her chair. She scrambles to her feet just as fast, but not before shooting you an embarrassed grin.

"That was awesome," you tell her. "Seriously."

Serena smiles back sweetly and nods her thanks. Then she returns to her seat and starts bringing up files.

"There's not much here," she says after a minute or two. "Almost everything is gone, just like the rest of the ship."

You scan the consoles alongside her, looking for clues. There has to be *something*. Anything.

"There," you say finally. You lean in and point to an embedded folder. "Those look like visual log entries."

"Deck cam footage," Serena agrees. "Yeah." She begins pulling them up. The files are small, the entries short. They fill a half dozen of the screens above you before she hits the PLAY button.

Whoa... did you finally find something useful? Find out *OVER ON PAGE 118*

You push START and the game roars to life. Music plays. Lights flash. A geometrically-arranged force of alien warships appears at the top of the screen, bearing down on your one tiny vessel.

Using the joystick you move left and right, dodging incoming missiles and firing back in turn. For several minutes you lose yourself in the game. But no matter how many of them you destroy, the colorful ships keep coming. They dive-bomb you through three successive waves, until your ship finally takes enough damage that it's blown to glowing white pieces.

The music turns sad for a moment, and then the Top 20 High Scores screen appears. You weren't even close. Absently you examine the list of scores, names and dates of play when something odd occurs to you.

The dates are all... wrong.

Serena's voice snaps you back to reality. "Andon! Come over here!"

You walk backward out of the room, still staring at the screen.
TURN TO PAGE 91

60

"Let's check it out," you whisper. Although when you think about it, you really don't know why you're whispering.

You poke your way into the pitch black alcove where Serena says she noticed movement. Things get even darker, if possible. You can't help but imagine what it would be like if your wrist-lamps went out. How terrible it would be to be completely, utterly alone. Swallowed by the blackness...

"OH!"

Serena's scream causes you to nearly jump out of your suit. You whip around and point your beam in her direction... just in time to see a disembodied hand float by.

"Is... is that..."

"No," you say, breathing a sigh of relief. "It's just a glove."

Your heart is still hammering in your chest as you reach the end of the alcove. It's a maintenance room, nothing more.

Serena looks up from her hand terminal. "Gravity's off in this part of the ship," she says. "I'm reading mostly vacuum, but there's still a hint of atmosphere."

"What does that mean?"

"It means that whatever happened here, it happened fast."

Good job being brave. *HEAD ON OVER TO PAGE 66*

You fly through another series of corridors until you notice an open door. Beyond it you find an elaborate stateroom. The furnishings here are formal yet personal. Opposite an immaculately made bed, a large desk of real wood is pushed up against one wall.

"This must be the Captain's Quarters," Serena hazards a guess. She points out a heavy brass sextant resting on small display stand. "Man, that must've cost a fortune."

You make a quick inventory of the captain's room. There's no diary or log, no real information you can actually use. A framed photo on the wall depicts the captain's wedding day. The bride and groom are laughing, frozen forever in the time-honored tradition of feeding each other their wedding cake. At the bottom, scrawled in a woman's handwriting, it reads:

April 1st - The most wonderful day of my life.
All of my love, Victoria

Awww," Serena coos. "That's sweet."

Built into the wall above the captain's bed is his personal terminal. You lean over and scan through a few screens of the ship's diagnostics. The Dauntless has two lifeboats, each of which would fit the entire crew. Neither of them have been jettisoned.

"Maybe he went down with the ship?" Serena shrugs.

"Maybe," you say. "But this ship isn't down yet."

BOOM!

Almost on cue the floor shifts uncomfortably beneath you. The Dauntless rattles with the reverberation of magnetic docking clamps, engaging themselves against the outer hull.

"Looks like our friends are finally here," you tell your co-pilot. "Let's go see what they want."

Let's rock. *TURN TO PAGE 70*

62

Your hands close over the firing sticks for the PDC's. At even your slightest touch the giant turret swivels satisfyingly beneath you. Your feet itch to work the pedals...

"Alright, go ahead." Reluctantly you let go. "See if you can hail them."

Serena is already connected to the network. She punches open a channel and puts it through to the console speakers.

"Unknown vessel this is the Dauntless," she calls into the mic. You look back at her and shrug.

"We have transponder and weapons lock on your ship," your co-pilot lies. "Please state your intentions."

At first there's no answer. Then, very faintly, a series of strange sounds and clicks reaches the back of your eardrums.

"This is the Dauntless," Serena repeats. "Please identif–"

Abruptly the sounds grow louder; a cacophony of strange, eerie wails and trailing shrieks of static. Through the viewport, you notice the ship coming around. It's still heading for the Dauntless, but now its nose is pointed directly in your direction.

"Uhhh... Serena?"

"Shhh!" your co-pilot tells you. She has an ear pressed to one speaker. "Hang on. I think I can make something out..."

If you want to wait it out a few more seconds, *TURN TO PAGE 102*
If you've waited long enough, jump in the cannon and *GO TO PAGE 40*

Another series of ramps opens up into a large area. Here you find the Dauntless's Reactor Room, and like everything else on the ship, it's impressive.

The power core itself glows a deep, luminescent blue. It's like nothing you've ever seen before. A glance at Serena tells the same story – she's just as in awe of the technology here as you are.

"Have you ever seen fuel cells like this?" she says, pointing to a stack of glowing blue orbs.

"No. Not even close."

You cross over a wide catwalk and approach the command console. Everything is in the green, but only barely. Screen after screen of raw data shows the Dauntless running at flank speed, taxing the engines to the absolute maximum. Temperatures are still high. It would take only a minimum of effort to implement an overload.

"Think we could rig this thing to destruct?" you ask Serena. "I mean, giving us enough time to make it back to the Kestrel first, of course?"

Your co-pilot seems lost in thought. "I don't know. By now we can both agree there's no one else on board. Still..."

"Still what?"

"There's still something I don't like about it. All these people, all of them so mysteriously gone. I just feel like we're missing something..."

You glance back at the command console. The fuel cells aren't the only thing that's unfamiliar. This is a tough one.

If you want to overload the power core and set the Dauntless on a destruct sequence, *GO TO PAGE 56*

If you think maybe you'd like to secure a path to the Kestrel first, *GO TO PAGE 28*

64

You smell the next corridor well before you see it. Smoke reaches your nostrils, and before long you're stepping over small bits of blackened debris.

"It's their ship!" Serena hisses, peering around the corner. She points to the jagged piece of hull the creatures cut away in order to enter the Dauntless. "We've gone in a big circle."

For a minute you stand in silence, just listening. Then ever so slowly, you approach the makeshift docking hatch and look inside. The boarding vessel is enormous. It's also empty. Ghastly green light emanates from control surfaces above and below. The screens are foreign, alien. There's nothing that you recognize, except for–

"That's a command terminal!"

Strangely enough, one of the Dauntless's command terminals rests on the boarding vessel's central console. A series of wires and strange connectors is somehow linking it to their ship. Your co-pilot steps in. You follow. It takes a few moments and some tinkering, but eventually Serena brings up one of the alien ship's screens. It's a bizarre mixture of glass and some kind of liquid.

"They connected their ship to the Dauntless!" Serena breathes. "Probably to access its main computer so they can find everything."

"And us," you add. Warily you check the corridor in both directions. Still nothing. Serena punches a few more commands into the pirated terminal. A bunch of information flashes by. Her face light up.

"What?"

"I can use this!" she cries suddenly. "Andon, I can access their information from here! The connection goes both ways. I can work their ship's controls... I can even see the mothership!"

Your co-pilot's fingers fly over the stolen console. As she does, the lights around you begin to change color. They go all different shades of green, some glowing brightly, others dimming down to near darkness. There's a hum from beneath you as Serena accesses more of the boarding ship's systems.

Then, just as suddenly, everything stops. The hum dies. Serena looks crestfallen.

"What happened?"

She points to the sickle-shaped vessel, now on the screen. "Their ship locked the terminal."

"So unlock it!"

"I can't," Serena says frantically. "I'd need the master override code to get back in. Only the captain of the Dauntless would have that code!"

You pause, and then suddenly a thought occurs to you.

"Well, not necessarily..."

Time to step up!

If you happen to know the captain's wedding date, take the month (as the tens column) and the year (as the ones column) and then *GO TO THAT PAGE* (For example: JUNE 5th would be page 65)

If you know the name of the ship's cat, use the chart below to add up all the letters in the word. When you have the total you can *GO TO THAT PAGE*

A = 1	F = 6	K = 11	P = 16	U = 21	Z = 26
B = 2	G = 7	L = 12	Q = 17	V = 22	Example:
C = 3	H = 8	M = 13	R = 18	W = 23	ANNA =
D = 4	I = 9	N = 14	S = 19	X = 24	1+14+14+1
E = 5	J = 10	O = 15	T = 20	Y = 25	= 30

If you don't know either of those things, or can't figure it out, *TURN TO PAGE 120*

66

You finally arrive at the Operations Deck. Serena gets right to work, plugging in the battery pack from the Kestrel. She's quickly able to power up most vital systems from the ship's mainframe. A short time later life support kicks in as the power core goes online.

"Great job," you tell her after a few minutes have passed. "How long before we can–"

"Actually, right now," Serena says, unfastening her helmet. You follow her lead, happy to be rid of the bulky headgear. Breathing deep, you fill your lungs. The air smells faintly of ozone and plastic, but compared to the canned air of your suit it tastes almost sweet.

"Life-support is already 84% restored," Serena tells you. "Temperature is 61 degrees and climbing."

"Any sign of the crew?"

Your co-pilot shakes her head. "No, but look at this."

One of the upper screens flips over to an external view. Serena dials up the magnification and a yellow, sickle-shaped object comes into focus.

"Another ship?"

"Yes."

The sickle-shaped object appears utterly motionless on screen. According to the sensors however, it's screaming full speed in your direction.

"How long?" you ask.

"They'll be here in less than half an hour," Serena answers. "And we already can't go any faster."

You chuckle, causing Serena to raise an eyebrow.

"This ship is The Dauntless," you explain. "Dauntless means 'courage'."

"So?"

"So then why were they running?"

Your gaze follows Serena's to the operations panel. None of the read-outs make any sense. Everything is foreign, from the shape of the ship to its hull signature. Even the engine readings are all wrong.

"That ship isn't from Earth," you say. "It wasn't built on Mars, or any of Jupiter's moons either."

Serena looks back at you blankly. "Then where is it from?"

"I don't know. But we'd better be ready for it when it gets here."

Better get moving. *TURN TO PAGE 76*

68

"Can you get in there?" you ask Serena, pointing out the narrow gap. "If so, maybe we can bring the engine temperature down a bit."

Serena doesn't hesitate. She wriggles through, and once in position you spend the next several minutes telling her which valves to open and which to close. Steam obscures your vision. Sweat drips from the line of your jaw. In the end though, you notice a difference. The temperature in your immediate vicinity rises as the overall engine temperature goes down.

"Good enough," you tell her. "Now get out of there before you burn up!"

The problem however, is that Serena doesn't move. Her arm is outstretched, reaching for another cluster of valves set deeper along the engine casing.

"Hand me those channel-locks," she tells you. "I think I can reach those last few handles."

The heat and noise have reached new levels of discomfort. The air itself is oppressive. You're not sure you should stay another minute, but you're also unsure that you've done enough. Still, you can't even see the valves Serena wants to close. You'd just have to take her word for it.

Yikes! This is a tough one.

If you hand Serena the channel-lock pliers, grit your teeth and *TURN TO PAGE 89*

If you think the both of you should probably get out of there, *GO TO PAGE 119*

The man steps in on you. You holster your weapon, ball your hand into a fist, and swing away.

With lightning speed, he ducks under it.

You never see the counter punch coming. It slams into your ribs like an electric shock, convulsing your muscles in a short, painful burst.

Angrily you swing again. This time the boxer dodges to one side. *Wham! Wham!* He throws two quick jabs that connect with your chin. Your head snaps back like a speedbag, that same electric feeling rattling your brain. When you look up again he's circling around for another series of attacks.

"BOXING PROGRAM DEACTIVATE!"

You recognize Serena's voice. A split-second later, the boxer disappears in a flash of light and static.

"NEXT PROGRAM?" a computerized voice calls from somewhere above you.

"No next program," your co-pilot says loudly. "Stand down."

You stand there at first just rubbing your jaw. Then you throw a few quick punches into the air and start shuffling your feet around.

"C'mon! I totally had him!"

Serena chuckles. "Yeah, okay. Except we don't have time to sit here watching you get beat up by a hologram." The incoming boarding ship leaps suddenly to mind. She makes a good point.

"Here," Serena says, "take this." She hands you a long, sleek rifle. You notice she's holding another. "Found them in a weapons locker, while you were playing around."

"Just sitting there, unlocked?"

She nods. "Like I said before, this place is strange."

Playtime's over, at least for now. Exit the gym and *TURN TO PAGE 61*

70

You creep forward in the direction of the noise, passing through a series of storage alcoves packed with various combat gear. A belt of grenades hanging from a hook grabs your attention. There are two types: concussion and high-explosive. You take some of each.

A couple of hallways later you stop in your tracks. The corridor is filled with black smoke. Bright orange sparks shower downward, bouncing off the deck like rain.

"They're cutting their way in."

The ship hasn't docked with the Dauntless at an external airlock. It's latched onto the side of the hull instead, like some kind of a space-remora.

Moments later a jagged piece of the hull drops inward with a loud clang. The smoke swirls, fades away, and then the first of the creatures steps into view.

The thing crawls more than walks through the white-hot hole in the Dauntless's hull, ducking to fit its bulk into the narrow space. It can't even come close to standing up straight. If it could, it would be well over eight feet tall.

Two more creatures follow it in, then a third. They're humanoid in shape, but with skin resembling a reptile's, or maybe the bark on a really gnarled tree. Strange metal plates appear to be fused to their skin of their torso, legs, and shoulders. Armor maybe, or something else.

You glance down at Serena. She's standing totally motionless, frozen in place. It's a lot to process.

"Need a minute?"

"Yeah," she breathes. Then she points over your shoulder. "But we don't have one."

When you turn back around the creatures have split up. Half of them are lumbering down the corridor in your direction. Instinctively you shrink back, gripping your rifle in one hand, palming the grenades in the other. You're not sure what to do next.

If you use the element of surprise, and your rifles, *FLIP TO PAGE 96*

If you throw a high-explosive grenade, *TURN TO PAGE 141*

If you roll a concussion grenade their way, *HEAD OVER TO PAGE 34*

If you'd rather back down the corridor and scramble for another option, *GO TO PAGE 79*

72

You don't move. You don't even breathe...

Serena screams as a water reclamation unit is torn from the wall beside her. One of the creatures has found you. You look to for a way to escape, but then two more of them step in, forming an impenetrable circle.

Maybe the monsters could sense your body heat. Or maybe they just have a good sense of smell. In any case, hiding was a bad idea. You're left with no way out, which unfortunately makes this

THE END

The creature is nearly upon you. With nothing else to do you and your co-pilot jump into the lifeboat and start looking for a place to hide.

The escape ship is long and box-shaped. Two tight rows of uncomfortable-looking seats make up the back of the vessel. You crouch down in the jump-seats behind the pilot and co-pilot's stations just as the creature reaches the lifeboat's airlock.

The thing pauses at the doorway in consideration. Its claws curve wickedly into sharp points. Its face is vaguely snout-like; jagged rows of teeth protrude beneath a series of cruel red eyes. Its breath is putrid. The smell settles over you almost physically, like a blanket of garbage.

For a long moment the creature seems satisfied that the boat is empty. Then, inexplicably, it moves inside. The small vessel cramps the monster even more, packing it from floor to ceiling. You and Serena hug yourselves into balls, curling against opposite bulkheads as the thing moves past the pilot's station and into the back of the lifeboat.

It reaches for something, over-extending itself...

You don't even think. In one fluid motion you spring upward, grab one of the ceiling handles, and swing the entire weight of your body into the creature's back. At the last moment you kick outward, striking it with two booted heels. It's like kicking a granite statue...

74

...it falls!

Already overextended, the creature sprawls forward into the back of the lifeboat, where it becomes temporarily wedged between the two tight rows of uncomfortable seats that make up each side.

"GO!"

Your co-pilot is already way ahead of you – moving with cat-like precision she's up and she's out. You spin past the door without looking back, and the second you're through the opening Serena slams the airlock closed behind you.

Beyond the double glass portholes you can see the creature scramble back to its feet. It whips around and shoots you a baneful glare, then starts charging straight back at the doorway...

An explosion of compressed air hits you full in the face as Serena punches the emergency launch. The creature's eyes go wide as the lifeboat propels it away from the Dauntless. Its mouth opens in a savage, silent scream as it grows smaller and smaller through the tiny viewport.

Then it explodes!

A beam of searing green energy originates from the enemy mothership, utterly consuming the lifeboat. You watch together in wonder, then breathe a long sigh of relief knowing how close you both came to being on board.

The adventure continues when you *TURN TO PAGE 54*

"Hang on a second," you tell Serena. "I have an idea."

Pulling your utility knife you cut and strip a thin length of wire from one of the purification control panels. Then, using the leftover grenades you found earlier, you rig a simple tripwire between the first two tanks.

Your co-pilot watches with interest, glancing up every now and then to look for signs of the enemy. You've just finished loosening the pins when the first of the big creatures shambles into view.

"Andon!" Serena whispers. "Hurry!"

Your fingers shake as you tie the knots. With the last one finished you pull the line taut and set it at knee level, which you guess to be ankle level for them.

"Hey!" you cry out when you're both safely in the next corridor. "Come on, over here!"

The few warning shots you fire off are unnecessary. You already have the creatures' attention. They bolt full speed in your direction, which turns out to be faster than you would've originally thought.

KA-BLAM!

The cisterns on either side of the monsters suddenly cave inward, collapsing around them in a rushing wave. Most of the high-explosive grenades' energy is absorbed by the water. The room begins fills rapidly from a combination of the shattered tanks and two broken water mains as you reach forward and engage both locks on the pressure doors.

"Think they'll drown?" Serena asks.

"No," you answer. "But they're definitely gonna need some towels."

TURN TO PAGE 107

76

The next part of the ship opens into a very long, rectangular room. Long metal pillars line both the left and right sides. In the center, a spinning cylinder of silver-white light immediately catches your eye.

You approach the pillar of light, mesmerized by its swaying, delicate movements. At times it appears to be moving very slowly. But then, without changing speed, you'd swear that it somehow started moving extremely fast.

"What is it?"

Serena's voice seems to come from someplace very distant, very far away. You blink your eyes a few times, and find that she's standing right next to you.

"I...I don't–"

Your hand trails over the translucent surface, which feels and looks like the smoothest glass. Without realizing it your fingers catch something. You look down and see a star-shaped depression set into the cylinder. Above the depression it reads: CTSTASIS

"That's it!" Serena cries. She points to the lines of long metal tubes. "We found the crew!"

You scan the two-dozen or so capsules along the walls. They don't look much like the Cryostasis tubes you've seen in your lifetime. Then again, there are similarities. Hundreds of tiny LED's flash along the length of each capsule, while flat black cables trail neatly away, disappearing beneath the floor.

When you look up again Serena is standing before an access terminal. She's lost in thought, biting the tip of one finger. It's a look you've seen before.

"Should I try to override the access code?" she asks. "I don't want to mess anything up."

You step up and examine the seal on one of the tubes. It doesn't look that complicated.

"I could just break the lock," you say with a shrug.

If you want Serena to run a bypass, *HEAD DOWN TO PAGE 21*

If breaking the locking mechanism sounds better, *FLIP OVER TO PAGE 82*

"Hit the yellow button!" you tell Serena. She looks apprehensive.

"You sure?"

"No, of course not! But hit it anyway."

Your co-pilot slams her hand down on the blinking yellow button. There's a whooshing sound, the room lights up, and the floor begins shifting beneath you.

"EMERGENCY OVERRIDE," a computerized voice booms down from somewhere overhead. "PLASMA INJECTION ASSEMBLY WILL BE PURGED IN 10 SECONDS."

"That good?" you ask.

"Yes! That's what we wanted."

You lean back against one of the panels in relief. But Serena is already pushing you toward the doorway.

"Being around here is *not* what we want," she tells you.

"TEN... NINE... EIGHT..."

Better not stick around for the rest of the countdown. *HEAD OVER TO PAGE 115*

78

You've had it with this ship, its mysteries, and now, its apparently crazy people.

"Enough is enough." You squeeze the trigger.

The round strikes the man square in the chest. Or at least, where his chest ought to be. Instead of hitting him however, it passes straight through his body and out the other side. The man is a hologram!

"BOXING PROGRAM DEACTIVATED," an unknown voice calls from overhead. Conveniently, the man dissolves – with a burst of noise and static – into a million dissipating pixels.

You breathe a long sigh of relief. But only one.

"FIREARMS TRAINING PROGRAM COMMENCING"

Wait? What?

"LETHALITY LEVEL: ONE-HUNDRED PERCENT"

A man materializes wearing full combat armor over a projectile deflection suit. You don't have combat armor. You don't have a deflection suit.

A woman appears beside him, then another man. They all have weapons identical to yours. They have cover.

They're aiming at you.

"Wait! Stop!" you scream. "Serena? Help!"

Unfortunately there's no help to be had here. For you at least, this is

---

THE END

The creatures may be big, but they also appear slow. They should be made even slower, you reason, by the fact the corridors are simply too narrow for them.

Taking advantage of this you back slowly away, keeping Serena behind you. You don't seem to be noticed as you enter into another part of the ship.

"This is crazy," Serena mutters in a low tone. "We have to get back to the Kestrel."

"Not until we figure out what these things are," you say with more confidence than you actually feel. "Besides, our orders are to sit tight until the Blackthorne gets here."

"If we're still here when it arrives."

After a short breather you drop down a ladder and continue exploring. You move slowly, cautiously, aware you could run into another one of the creatures at any moment. Eventually you're dumped into a large room that reminds you of a maintenance garage. Everything smells of metal and sulfur and grease.

TURN TO PAGE 109

80

The outer door cycles. The airlock is flushed. It happens wordlessly, soundlessly. Eventually the cycle resets itself and the pressure doors slide open with the sinister hiss of hydraulics.

Serena is gone.

You stumble forward a few steps, your eyes glazed over. A few steps more and your legs give out. You fall to your knees.

"UNAUTHORIZED PERSONNEL DETECTED"

You can barely hear the words. Don't even notice the sound of the pressure doors slamming closed behind you.

"AIRLOCK WILL BE AUTO-PURGED IN 10 SECONDS..."

In your grief you've wandered a few steps too far. But it doesn't even matter. And that's because this is

---

THE END

With Serena behind you, you step into a narrow service corridor. Everything is dark and feels very cramped. You've never really been claustrophobic, but there's a first time for everything.

"Follow that network conduit," Serena instructs you, pointing to a thick yellow cable. "That should lead to the mainframe."

You move slowly. Cautiously. The twin beams of your wrist-lamps dance ahead as you make your way deeper into the ship. Although your suit keeps you at a comfortable temperature, the corridor is very cold. A razor-thin crust of ice coats just about everything.

"Uh... Andon?"

"What is it?" you ask.

Serena points into the darkness of a tiny side-passage.

"Something just moved down there..."

If you're brave enough to investigate the side passage *TURN TO PAGE 60*

If you think continuing straight to Operations would be a wiser idea, *TURN TO PAGE 66*

82

You pick one of the tubes and stand next to it. The locking mechanism is electronic and relatively small.

"Here goes nothing."

Raising a fist you smash down hard on the backlit lock panel. The display flickers wildly for a moment, then goes totally dark. You thumb the release mechanism. There's the hiss of hydraulics, and the whole thing pops out and upward.

TURN TO PAGE 92

You move into the kitchen, determined to find something resembling a decent beverage. The coffee on the Kestrel has historically been abysmal. Besides, you're parched.

Most of the kitchen equipment is machinery you recognize. A few things however, you don't. Everything appears compact, more concise. You push open the square door of a recycling container to find it clean and empty.

"Found some!"

Serena beams victoriously as she tosses you a bulb of black coffee. Your co-pilot has already popped the heating mechanism at the bottom of the bulb, instantly bringing the drink to a perfect 175 F.

"Oh man," she says, savoring her first sip. "It's just as fresh as the rest of the ship!"

She's right. It's fantastic. You take a moment to enjoy it, then start checking the rest of the kitchen. On the wall is a set of gleaming cutlery. You pick a knife off the magnetic block and admire its razor sharpness.

"Hey, wanna try this?"

Your co-pilot is holding up two plastic tubes she removed from a refrigeration unit. One is black, one is blue.

"What is it?"

She shrugs. "Don't know. But they smell okay."

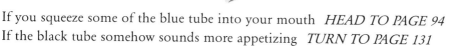

If you squeeze some of the blue tube into your mouth *HEAD TO PAGE 94*
If the black tube somehow sounds more appetizing *TURN TO PAGE 131*
If 'smells okay' doesn't sound like the right criteria for ingesting some unknown goo, declare the coffee break over and *TURN TO PAGE 36*

84

Your first string of shots miss, but they're not far off. Consulting the HUD you fire again, walking the deadly line of plasma bolts straight toward the enemy ship. You're almost there, when all of a sudden...

"The guns are jammed!"

Serena points out three flashing orange lights on your console. The fourth one is red. None of the cannons will fire.

Above you, the boarding ship is coming around. It noses over in your direction and begins bearing down on you.

"OUT!" you scream, detaching yourself from the turret. You grab Serena's hand and pull her through the hatch. As you scramble for cover, the PDC station behind you floods with a sickening green light...

Hurry up! *TURN TO PAGE 57*

You wriggle your way through the narrow passage, which isn't much more than a utility corridor. After stepping over a bunch of sheathed cable and power transformers, you emerge in the Dauntless's Torpedo Command room.

The screens here are already on. Various tracking systems have the jagged enemy ship targeted and already locked. It's as if someone was previously trying to get a firing solution, but had to leave before the ship got in range. It's more than in range now.

"Think we should?" Serena says, reading your mind.

You examine the console. You're familiar with a lot of different weapon systems; although this one appears very advanced, it really boils down to two things: point and shoot. And in this case, the pointing part seems to have been already done for you.

"There are four tubes loaded," you tell your co-pilot. "Two are heat-seekers. Two high-explosive."

"That's good, right?"

"Very. But I can only launch two at a time."

You're confident the high explosive torpedoes would tear the enemy ship in two... if you could hit with them. Then you consider the heat-seekers. Launched from this close a range, they would be very deadly. At the same time however, you don't even know if the enemy ship has a heat signature at all.

"Here goes nothing," you tell Serena.

If you launch two high-explosive torpedoes, *TURN TO PAGE 87*

If you'd rather hit them with the heat-seekers, *TURN TO PAGE 55*

If you think it might be best to launch one of each torpedo type, *TURN TO PAGE 25*

86

Your heart still pounds as the lift rises quickly through the Dauntless's decks. You left a few of those things behind you, but more of them could be anywhere. Above or below.

Eventually the lift shudders to a stop and the doors slide open. When you step out, you're at the maintenance exit of what looks to be a very high end, very spacious lounge.

The room is much bigger than it needs to be. A serving area sits off to one side, filled with multi-colored glasses and decanters. Couches and chairs are set in comfortable arrangements throughout the room, looking very sleek and neat.

"This place keeps getting stranger and stranger," Serena says. "I mean, look at this–"

The lights go out. It happens quickly, plunging you into total blackness. A few seconds later, the darkness is punctuated by the sound of shattered glass.

"Serena!" you cry out. From somewhere up ahead you can hear a muffled response. Behind you; the rumblings of a snarl or growl, low and close. Far too close.

Do you rush forward and try to help Serena? If so, *TURN TO PAGE 32*

Or do you freeze and try to remain utterly silent? If so, *TURN TO PAGE 43*

You've had enough running, enough hiding. If ever there was an opportunity to end this thing, it's here and now.

Slamming the launch controls, you fire two high-explosive torpedoes at the enemy ship. The missiles scream out of the Dauntless from somewhere beneath your feet. Burning brightly in the darkness, you watch with grim satisfaction as they streak directly toward their intended target.

The enemy ship comes alive almost immediately. For the first time since it arrived, you get a sense of alarm and urgency on their part. The sickle-shaped warship turns on its axis, firing twin green beams that explode one of the torpedoes. The second missile however, is already too close. It slams into the side of the alien ship with a tremendous explosion.

"You did it!" Serena cheers. A thousand glimmering shards break free from the other vessel, blooming outward from the scorched, gaping hole. Still, the ship moves of its own power. It shudders visibly it rockets away, slowing to hang back another few thousand kilometers from the Dauntless.

"Maybe it's crippled," you say with more confidence than you feel. "If we're lucky."

A noise reaches your ears, faint at first, then louder. It's coming from the corridor behind you.

"Let's go Marine," you tell your co-pilot. "We are leaving!"

Retreat through the opposite exit and *TURN TO PAGE 63*

88

You leap aboard the handtruck's operating platform and kick it to life. It floats a half foot above the deck, zipping rapidly forward under your command.

The creatures are coming even faster now. You line up the truck with them. Accelerating quickly through normal operating levels, you thumb the yellow switch that allows you even more speed...

But then something goes wrong. A large bump of air changes your trajectory, and nearly throws you from the platform. You stay on, but it's a struggle just to regain control. This is a much newer model, you realize. You're unfamiliar with much of the console. Maybe if you could just–

"Andon!"

By the time Serena screams it's already too late. Your handtruck blasts through a biohazard container, spilling fuel rods everywhere. Some of them shatter. All of them glow a sickly, luminescent blue...

Klaxon horns blare from every direction as radiation floods the chamber. Pressure doors slide shut, locking you in, keeping the rest of the ship safe while you, Serena, and your two new friends remain quarantined to the spill-zone... forever.

Good try anyway! But regrettably for you, this is

THE END

"Here... just be careful."

Your co-pilot grabs the tool and transfers it to her other hand. You cross your fingers as she begins working on the far set of valves. Almost immediately the room fills with a thick white haze. You feel the pressure building, and you know instantly that you made the wrong decision.

"Turn it back! Turn it back!" you shout over the noise. "Wrong one!"

But it's too late. Serena is past hearing you as she slumps over from the heat. Yanking hard you manage to pull her free of the crawlspace, but the damage is already done. She's closed the wrong valves, and this time the temperature keeps rising and rising.

Unable to fix what happened, or even think straight, you sink to the hard metal floor of Engineering. As the turbine screams into the unrecoverable zone, it looks like this is

THE END

90

You decide to duck under the machine one last time. Patiently you wait for just the right moment, trying to gauge speed and distance and the ever-shortening gap between you and the mechanized loader. At the last possible second you leap out of the way, just before an arc of molten plasma sears a hole right through your flight suit (and you!)

"We're leaving!" you announce unnecessarily. Grabbing your co-pilot's hand, you yank her into the opposite corridor.

"Remind me not to go ever back there," you say aloud.

"Don't ever go back there," Serena tells you.

The corridor is long and dark and *OPENS INTO PAGE 66*

You enter the Life Support station just as Serena finishes punching a long series of buttons. "It's not Engineering," she shrugs, "but this is the next best thing."

Before her, panel after panel goes from dark to light. There's an explosion of light and sound as the ship's power is restored, followed by the hum of dozens of air scrubbers striving to work overtime.

"INFINITY," Serena says with a smirk.

"What?"

"That was their bypass code," she explains. She shakes her head. "Pretty lame code if you ask me."

"Oh. Yeah. Uh, when can we get out of these helmets?"

For several minutes you hear nothing but the roar of the air scrubbers working to oxygenate the environment. At last Serena motions for you to take off your helmet. Streams of crisp, medicinal-smelling air flooding the room wash over you.

"Gravity systems are in the green," Serena tells you. "We should be good for now."

With the lights on, the ship looks different – all whitewash and polish and shine. The walls are still slick with rapidly melting frost, but everything is clean, beautiful. New technology seems to be everywhere.

Ahead of you is a wide metal archway, opening into a much larger room.

"Come on," you say, stepping forward. "They're not paying us by the hour."

FLIP BACK TO PAGE 11

92

The Cryostasis tube opens! For a few seconds all you can see is fog and moisture as they swirl from the cylinder. Then the mist dissipates, and you're left staring at...

Absolutely nothing.

"Seriously?" Serena asks no one in particular. "This place is weird." She moves beside you and gently closes the Cryotube.

"If the crew's not here they've got to be somewhere else," you reason. "But we've got bigger problems. That other ship is going to catch us soon, so we'd better keep moving."

Keep moving.

Head through the big wide exit when you *TURN TO PAGE 115*
Or you can take the smaller corridor off to one side by *HEADING TO PAGE 132*

You stand there silently for another moment before loudly clearing your throat. Nothing happens.

"Hey! You!"

The figure at the Comm Station remains utterly motionless. Either they're ignoring you, or sleeping, or the audio sensors in their helmet have been switched off.

Serena's face goes dark with an even grimmer thought. "Maybe they're... you know..."

Thinking back to the ship chasing the Dauntless you realize there isn't much time. You cross the room noisily and rap the person hard on the helmet. It echoes emptily. Lifting the visor, you show Serena what you already suspected:

The suit is empty.

"Figures," your co-pilot says. Serena helps you drag the suit away from the Comm station and then slides into the chair. She starts pushing buttons.

"Let's see where this ship has been... and what it's been up to."

Check out the Comm Logs by *GOING TO PAGE 124*

94

Taking the tube you squeeze some of the blue goo into your mouth. Instantly you regret it. Your tongue goes numb and you can no longer feel your lips. Your entire face feels flush, like you just ran back-to-back marathons.

"Aaaaa... Ack!"

You can't speak. Or even move, for that matter. Serena's eyes go wide as the sun, and then darkness creeps in from the corners of your vision. Suddenly you're falling...

When you come to, you find yourself strapped into the jump-seat of the Kestrel. Serena's flying. She looks worried.

"Uh, hey..." she says when she notices you. "Welcome back."

Your head is a lead weight. Your mouth feels like you ate an entire can of wall paste.

"Wha... what happened?"

"Protein overdose," Serena says, "as far as I can tell. I barely got you off that ship. You'll be okay, I think, but we really need to get you checked out."

Well you're alive, at least for now. But unfortunately, with your mission failed, this means it's

THE END

"See if you can take the console," you tell her. "Getting control of this auxiliary bridge is important. We need to know what happened here."

Your co-pilot answers with her fingertips. Only a minute later however, she abruptly stops typing.

"UNAUTHORIZED ACCESS DETECTED. LOCKOUT PROCEDURE INITIATED."

You glance up, as if you could actually see the voice overhead. Or even plead with it.

"What's it saying? What does that mean?"

Again Serena doesn't answer. She's typing frantically now. Her face is drawn with worry.

"Serena! Talk to me!"

"I– I can't..." she stammers. "It's locking me out! I'm trying to get around it, but the computer's anticipating everything I do!"

CLICK! Both exits to the room sound with the dull thunk of a powerful electromagnetic locking mechanism. You're not going anywhere, anytime soon...

Oh man, that's not good. Better flip a coin!

If it comes up HEADS, *TURN TO PAGE 45*

If the coin comes up TAILS instead, *FLIP TO PAGE 58*

96

You're not even sure if your weapons will work on these creatures. But they're coming fast, so you aim and fire.

You let out a few staccato bursts from your rifle. The small corridor is quickly filled with smoke and debris. Beneath you, Serena's strange black weapon has a much different effect. It emits a steady yellow beam of concentrated light that sweeps left and right in a razor sharp, deadly arc.

Inhuman screams echo from within the chaos. Two green beams slice back in your direction; apparently the creatures have weapons as well. The beams sweep back and forth, as if searching for you with a life of their own. Instinctively you duck for cover behind a bulkhead.

Abruptly the fighting stops. For a few seconds there's nothing but smoke and silence, and then Serena grabs your hand and pulls you through a narrow side corridor.

"C'mon! They can't fit through here!"

TURN BACK TO PAGE 85

You watch helplessly as one of the creatures storms by. You still haven't taken a breath when the second one lumbers through, moving so painstakingly slow you're pretty sure your lungs will burst.

The second it's gone Serena ducks down and crawls beneath a nearby water reclamation unit. You follow, but you can barely fit. Shimmying along the dirt-streaked floor you feel frightened and vulnerable. If the creatures found you now, there would be nothing you could do. No way to even defend yourself, trapped in this tiny space with your arms at your sides...

Suddenly you notice your co-pilot is no longer in front of you. A hand shoots back toward your face, you grab it, and Serena pulls you into the next area.

You feel like a pancake, but you made it. *TURN TO PAGE 107*

98

You make one last effort to break free of the loadbot's iron grip. Unfortunately, you don't have the strength or power to keep it from slamming you into the closest container.

The last thing you hear is Serena's very late attempt at a last-minute warning. You slump to the floor of the Cargo bay, hoping it's not but eventually realizing that this is probably

THE END

"Ninety-Nine," you say. "The Comm Room radio was set to that old dummy frequency, remember?"

Serena's face lights up with recognition as she punches a few buttons on the touchscreen. A sound begins transmitting over the console's speakers. It's deep, noisy and guttural. A series of clicks and grunts rises up from the distortion in the background.

"What do we say?"

"Tell them to back off," you say, "or we're using the master control to override the power core and put the Dauntless in a ten-second destruct sequence."

Serena looks back at you wide-eyed. She's as white as a ghost.

"We're not *really* going to do that," you tell her with a nervous smile. "Relax."

But before your co-pilot can transmit anything, a low voice floats up over the channel. A human voice.

"...of the Alexa, representative of the Mars-Jupiter Alliance," a woman calls out mechanically. "Current transponder codes identify you as the Codec-class Kestrel. If you require assistance, Kestrel, please respond." The message goes on to repeat itself from the beginning. "This is Jules Howe, captain of the Alexa, representative of the Mars-Jupiter Alliance..."

"The Alexa is here!" Serena cries. "Or at least she's nearby."

You're not nearly as excited as your co-pilot. Being stranded on the Dauntless is the last thing you want, but the second to last thing would be to be indebted to some small-time captain from the MJA. Besides, you're not exactly sure what would happen when they got here.

"Our orders are to wait for the Blackthorne," you remind Serena. "Calling the Alexa might be a bad idea."

"It also might be our only chance to get off this ship alive," she shoots back.

You let out a long, deep breath. It's a tough call.

If you decide to radio the Alexa for help, *GO BACK TO PAGE 17*

If you'd rather not involve the Mars-Jupiter Alliance, take your chances by *FLIPPING TO PAGE 103*

100

A set of pure white double-doors opens into the Dauntless's Sick Bay. Three pristine examination tables stand surrounded by an array of complicated medical systems. Lights flash. Unintelligible readouts scroll by. Everything looks highly advanced – better than anything you've ever seen in the EWC fleet.

"Who are these people?" you breathe. You pick out a gleaming tool from a table of surgical instruments. It's immaculate. Feeling immediately like you've done something wrong, you place it neatly back in its row.

"I don't know," Serena says admiringly, "but I like them." She runs one hand over a counter top and holds her palm up to you. It comes back without a speck of dust.

THUMP!

A tall medical cabinet near Serena suddenly rattles violently. She takes a step closer to you.

"Now *that* I don't like," your co-pilot says.

Do you investigate the cabinet? If so *HEAD TO PAGE 46*

If the impending arrival of an enemy boarding vessel has you too spooked already, leave the Sick Bay and *TURN TO PAGE 14*

We don't have time for this, you think. Not with the other ship coming.

Putting your weapon away, you duck under the man's punch and bolt for the opposite exit. If this guy wants to follow you, or raise an alarm, great. Maybe you can get a hold of the ship's captain. Maybe you and your co-pilot can finally get some answers.

"Andon!"

You whip around. As you'd hoped, Serena has followed your lead. But then you notice something else... the man is gone! It's like he totally dematerialized, the second you stepped off the gym floor.

"He was just a training program," Serena says breathlessly. "A hologram."

You can't help but laugh. "I probably should've figured that out."

As Serena catches up you notice she's carrying something in each hand. She holds out a rifle, sleek and long. You take it, staring back at her incredulously.

"Storage locker," she tells you, by means of explanation. "C'mon, there's little time."

Serena's Right. *TURN TO PAGE 61*

102

"I got it!" Serena cries. "I think it's saying..."

Two dark holes in the bottom of the enemy ship suddenly flare to life. They glow with a sickly green luminescence, growing brighter and brighter until–

THWAP!

There's a rush of heat and light, followed by a deafening roar as the twin beams rip through the PDC's armor plating. You eyesight is thoroughly obliterated. And that's probably a good thing, because then you don't have to watch as you, Serena, and the entire cannon assembly are sucked out into the frozen void of space...

Sorry, this looks like

THE END

"Forget it," you tell Serena. "The Alexa is an interceptor, it's not even Frigate-class. It probably couldn't help us if it wanted to. I'm not risking anyone else's life right now."

Your co-pilot looks forlorn, but reluctantly she nods in agreement.

"Besides," you tell her, "the Blackthorne should almost be here."

At those words, Serena looks infinitely more hopeful. Her hands move over the console again, jacking up the volume and filling the channel with loud, obnoxious feedback. You cringe and clamp your hands over your ears as it rings horribly up and down your spine.

"Let them chew on that," she says smugly. You watch as she jams the comm switch in the open position. "It looked like they had big ears anyway."

TURN TO PAGE 107

104

You take a half-step back, raise your service pistol, and take aim. Then you squeeze the trigger.

PING!

Nothing happens.

You fire again, and again after that. Each time the round bounces harmlessly off the loadbot's titanium alloy and carbon-fiber body. The machine doesn't slow down, it doesn't speed up. It just keeps coming.

"Serena!" you shout helplessly. "I can't–"

All air is forced from your lungs as the half-ton robot slams into you from the side. Caught between its outstretched arms, it shoves you inexorably backward. Struggling does nothing. You may as well be trying to move a mountain!

You're in trouble! Roll one die (or just think of a random number from 1 to 6)
If the number is a 3 or 4, *TURN TO PAGE 98*
If the number is a 1, 2, 5 or 6, *TURN TO PAGE 142*

You're a few feet behind the creature when your foot suddenly catches something. You trip!

There's nothing to break your fall other than the monster itself. You knock into it as you sprawl to the floor, hoping to at least shove it off balance. It doesn't even budge. It's like trying to move an enormous boulder, only this boulder has three rows of savage-looking teeth.

Long and yellowed and jagged, those teeth bear down on you as you scramble backward on all fours. The creature towers over you, hissing from its raw, fetid throat. For a dangerous moment, you nearly roll over and retch. You're still being punched in the face with smells from another world, when suddenly–

The room flares a blinding yellow with the strange beam of Serena's rifle. You watch the creature's eyes go wide, and what might be four distinct pupils shrink down to virtually nothing. It can't see!

Your co-pilot's hand clamps over your wrist and jerks you to your feet. You resist the urge to look back as you run, the creature's inhuman roar still assailing your ears as you bolt down a cluster of wide service ramps.

You owe Serena another one. *HEAD BACK TO PAGE 23*

106

"INFINITY!"

Your fingers fly through the bypass code and you slam down the override. The voice overhead stops. The pressure doors slide open as the cycle is reversed, and Serena flies into your arms.

There was just one second left on the countdown. You can't help thinking how much it's just like in the movies.

"You remembered!" your co-pilot exclaims, thrilled to be still breathing oxygenated air. "And hey," she beams, "where'd you learn to type that fast?"

"Guess I had a good teacher," you smirk back.

Together you bid good riddance to the airlock zone and head deeper into the ship.

Nice work. *HEAD TO PAGE 61*

You bolt down the next corridor, which ends abruptly in a wide cargo lift. You can hear the creatures behind you, coming up fast, crashing through whatever happens to be in their way.

"Get in!" you yell, as Serena almost turns around to look. Once inside fear grips you. The doors aren't closing...

After what feels like forever, the heavy doors of the turbo lift finally slide shut. Your hands are shaking. Your nerves are fried. Your co-pilot's finger hovers over operations panel.

"Up or down?" Serena asks.

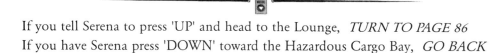

If you tell Serena to press 'UP' and head to the Lounge, *TURN TO PAGE 86*

If you have Serena press 'DOWN' toward the Hazardous Cargo Bay, *GO BACK TO PAGE 18*

108

"Roll the dial," you tell Serena. "They've got to be transmitting on something short-range, right?"

She works the controls. The room is filled with chirps, beeps, and various levels of space-static. Nothing much comes of it, until Serena stops on something that sounds low and guttural. There are sounds underneath the static. You'd swear you can hear a snort, or maybe a grunt.

"Stop. There."

The noises get louder. Your co-pilot makes a few adjustments, and things get clearer. Then, just as you're about to pick something up, a whole row of lights on the console start flashing brightly.

"What's that?"

The only answer you get is the look of terror on Serena's face. Her eyes go wide...

Roll a single die (or just pick a random number from 1 to 6)

If the number is a 3 or a 5, *HEAD OVER TO PAGE 27*

If the number is a 1, 2, 4, or 6, *FLIP DOWN TO PAGE 127*

The Machine Shop on the Dauntless is the only place you've seen that isn't neat. Tools hang everywhere. Ship parts lay scattered in various heaps across the floor. You see a half-dismantled maintenance bot, and a lift engine in so many pieces you doubt it could ever be put back together. Serena goes to pick up a hammer drill when, all of a sudden, you detect movement on the other side of the room.

One of the creatures lumbers in. For once luck is on your side – its back is toward you. Serena raises her rifle but you silently wave her away.

Grabbing a solid length of titanium pipe, you attempt to sneak up on it...

How clumsy are you? Roll one die (or just think of a random number from 1 to 6)

If the number comes up as a 1, *TURN TO PAGE 105*

If the number is a 2, 3 or 4, *TURN TO PAGE 135*

If the number is a 5 or 6, *TURN TO PAGE 130*

110

"CT STASIS," you say aloud. Serena's eyebrows come together as she just looks at you.

"It's a key," you explain. Gently you turn the star-shaped object over a few times in your hand. "It goes in that strange tube we found, back in Cryostasis."

You don't wait for an answer. Already you're moving, sprinting back to the long rectangular chamber. The two rows of cryo-tubes stand idle against the wall, all of them closed. The cylinder in the middle of the room still spins with a silvery-white glow.

You approach the column of light and find the star-shaped depression. The glass key fits perfectly into the lock. There's a flash of light, brighter than anything you've ever experienced in your life. You have the sensation of flying, of leaving your body for a brief shining moment... and then suddenly you're in the room again, and the light is gone.

Everything's changed.

"Welcome," a friendly voice calls out. "And most of all, thank you."

You look up. You and Serena are surrounded by people. They're all wearing yellow and black jumpsuits, with the Dauntless insignia on them. They stand around you in ring. Every one of them is smiling.

"What... who?"

"You're the crew!" Serena cries. She whirls in a circle. "So you *were* in Cryo Stasis!"

The man who spoke earlier – the captain – beams down at her. "Cryo *Temporal* Stasis," he corrects her. "We weren't just frozen in the physical world, we were also frozen in time."

"So that's what the 'CT' was for!" you think aloud. "And that's why the tubes were empty!"

The man pats the glass cylinder in the center of the room. You notice that it's no longer swirling with light.

"But how..." Serena jumps in. "How could..."

"It's a long story," he says, holding his hands up in a placating gesture. "Let's just say we're from a place where voyages such as this are possible."

"So you're from the future," you say aloud. It's not a question, it's a statement. For a moment the rest of the crew appears slightly uncomfortable. The captain just looks at you and winks.

"We were attacked on our way back to Earth," the man says. "Or as far as you're concerned, future-Earth." He pauses as if trying to decide what more to say. "Our bridge controls were damaged when the Waer'maer ambushed us. We were no longer able to steer the ship."

"The *Waer'maer*? You mean those things?" Serena asks.

"Yes, those. I believe you met them."

You're suddenly struck with an alarming thought. "Wait! They're still here! Some of them are still on the–"

"No, not any longer," the captain assures you. "My crew took care of them while you were, um, recovering." He smiles again. "Please sit back and relax for now. We'll be returning you to your ship shortly."

A few of the crew members clear their throats. The captain smirks.

"Oh yes, I almost forgot. The crew would like it if you autographed our bridge, General Mercer." He turns to face Serena. "You too, Colonel Valentine."

General? Colonel?

"Autographs?"

"Yes, of course," the captain answers, as if it were nothing. "It's an honor and a privilege to meet the two heroes responsible for saving humankind."

The entire crew beams down at you. Serena is absolutely bewildered.

"You knew we were coming," you theorize. "You already knew this whole thing would happen."

The captain raises an eyebrow. He looks genuinely impressed.

"Let's just say that time is a very funny thing." The man smirks again, then motions you toward a doorway.

You walk through the Dauntless's well-lit, well-loved corridors. With the crew present, you and Serena sign a portion of their bridge. They applaud you, loudly. It's all very surreal.

112

"We'd better get you back to the Kestrel," the captain says eventually. "The temporal displacement cells are almost recharged, and we have someplace else to be."

"Some *time* else," Serena corrects him, finally catching on. The captain tips an imaginary hat to her cheerfully.

A few minutes and too many handshakes later, you and your co-pilot are back on your ship. It feels good. Almost like home. The captain of the Dauntless appears on your viewscreen one last time and bids you farewell. You reach down to fire the engines, and by the time you look up again the Dauntless is gone.

A row of lights blinks along your console. A large blip has appeared at the edge of your radar.

"The Blackthorne is finally here," Serena says, and not without a hint of sarcasm. "The Commodore is going to want a full report."

"Yes," you agree with your co-pilot. "I'm pretty sure he will..."

CONGRATULATIONS!
YOU HAVE REACHED THE ULTIMATE ENDING!

In recognition for taking up the gauntlet, let it be known to fellow adventurers that you are hereby granted the title of:

Master of Time and Space!

You may go here: **www.ultimateendingbooks.com/extras.php** and enter code:

KY34970

for tons of extras, and to print out your Ultimate Ending Book Three certificate!

And for a special sneak peek of Ultimate Ending Book 4, *JUMP TO PAGE 143*

The computer terminal explodes! You shield your eyes as chunks of glass and plastic fly in every direction. Small flames rise from the smoking, jagged hole.

You look over and... Serena is still there!

The countdown has stopped. The lights on the airlock's mag-doors have gone dark. With all of your strength you yank them apart, and Serena flies into your arms, hugging you. Crying.

"Let's get out of here right now," you say reassuringly. It can't happen quickly enough. Four corridors and three sets of pressure doors later, the airlock is a fading memory. Your body however, still shakes with adrenalin.

Looks like you have a new lucky coin! *TURN TO PAGE 61*

114

You line the rifle up perfectly with the creature. It's too big to miss. You squeeze the trigger...

Unbelievably it moves, and with an unnerving, otherworldly speed. The high ceilings of the machine shop allow it to scramble away as round after round from your rifle explode against the inside of the Dauntless's hull.

A hole appears. A big hole. The force of the resulting vacuum hurls tools, debris, and metal containers straight at the already weakened break, and the hull rips even further open from the repeated impacts.

You grab onto something. But it's no use. As the bulkhead collapses the whole side of the room comes apart and the entire contents of the Machine Shop are flung into space. The air is forced from your chest as the cold, blackness of the void finally embraces you.

Sorry, but this is

THE END

After another short series of corridors you arrive at the Communications Room.

"Alright!" Serena cries out. Pushing forward excitedly, she starts to brush past you. "This is where we can find out–"

You restrain her with one arm and put a finger to your lips. "Shhh!" Your co-pilot catches on and stops in her tracks. She follows your gaze into the room.

There's someone in there.

A person is seated at the Comm Station, their back to you. Their hands rest on the controls. Whoever it is, they're wearing a full environmental suit.

"Finally," Serena whispers. "Now we get some answers."

"Hold on," you whisper back. "They might not exactly be friendly."

"So... what do you suggest?"

If you call out to the person, *TURN TO PAGE 93*

If you'd rather restrain them first, and talk afterward, *FLIP DOWN TO PAGE 128*

116

Enough!

It's one word... a simple, small word, but it's a word that sticks out solemnly in your mind. You've had enough of these things already. You've especially had enough of them screwing things up for you.

You stand motionless while the creature bears down on you. In fact, you move toward it. You sprint forward, along the catwalk, as if to meet it halfway. The thing's eyes change as it realizes what you're about to do, but by then it's already too late.

Just before the creature plows into you, you dive into its legs. It strikes you hard, knocking you sideways to the grated metal floor. But without its footing, it's unable to stop. The creature's momentum carries it over the low railing, flipping it – arms still flailing wildly – into the darkness of the level below.

You don't stop to admire your handiwork. Already you're pulling Serena out of the corridor she'd already chosen and ushering into a much different one.

"The Kestrel is this way."

Everything flies by. Neither of you say a word, legs tumbling beneath you as you run full-tilt through the Dauntless's abandoned halls. Three minutes later you're back at the original airlock. Relief floods through you as you see your ship again. The Kestrel is untouched, unoccupied.

You and Serena fly through the docking tube.

"Get her running. Fast."

Serena works the launch sequence faster than anything you've ever seen her do before. The ship's ready lights blink green as you seal the airlock and disengage the docking clamps. Ever so slowly, the Kestrel floats away from the Dauntless. You slap your co-pilot's hand away when she goes for the throttle.

"No. They'll see."

The drift away from the Dauntless is agonizingly slow. It's impossible to know how long you have before the core goes molten. A nightmare scenario plays itself out in your mind; the Kestrel, torn apart by the resulting explosion, just on the verge of being clear.

Serena's hands close over a different set of controls. Using short bursts of the rotational thrusters, she keeps the Dauntless between you and the alien mothership. It's a neat trick. It might even keep you hidden, at least for a while.

Without warning, a voice crackles over the comm.

"Kestrel this is Commodore Garriott of the EWC Blackthorne. We are incoming – ETA four and a half minutes. Please respond."

You see the enemy ship abruptly begin rotating. Your sensor panel starts blinking in a dozen places. The heat levels on the Dauntless are well beyond critical levels.

"Punch it."

Serena fires the Kestrel's engines at full burn. You pull rapidly away from both ships, in the direction of the Blackthorne. Seconds later, there's a brilliant burst of white light, followed by an even more sinister explosion of green. Both ships are vaporized. You made it!

Back on the Blackthorne, Commodore Garriott scratches his beard at your report. There are some details he still finds troubling. For one, the complete lack of the Dauntless's crew. For another, the fact that the Dauntless doesn't exist in any fleet's record. Anywhere.

For you and Serena though, most of this is inconsequential. Whatever was chasing the Dauntless was inevitably bound for Earth. And together, you stopped them.

Congratulations on a job well done!

THE END

118

Up on the screens of the Secondary Command bridge, you get your first real glimpse of the Dauntless's crew. They're normal men and women, moving through well lit corridors and wearing crisp, black and yellow jumpsuits. Everything looks clean, unblemished. But there's something wrong.

"They're hurrying."

As Serena advances through the recording, you notice an increased sense of urgency. The corridors empty out as crew members man their specific stations. Alarm lights paint the ship's decks in flashing red.

"Why isn't there any sound?"

Your co-pilot shrugs. She tries adjusting a few settings but it makes no difference. Back on the silent world of the Dauntless's screens, smoke begins to appear. You can see damage occurring in certain parts of the vessel, especially near what you perceive to be the ship's engines.

"They're being attacked," Serena says needlessly. "But by who?"

One of the screens abruptly goes dark. Another one however, cuts to a view of the main bridge. It's a graceful elongated circle of polished white, filled with crewmembers working frantically to save their ship. In the center of the room is the captain's chair. A man stands beside it, gripping one arm for leverage as he points to various stations all around him. You can only imagine what he's saying as he silently barks out orders.

Shortly after that the recordings stop. The screens all go blank.

"Wait," you say. "Go back a bit."

Serena rewinds the recording. You reach out and advance it manually, finally stopping at a moment where one of the bridge's main screens are visible.

"Enhancing," Serena says, reading your mind.

At 5x zoom you can finally see it: there's a ship on the other screen. Long and curved, it looks like a sickle. Or a scythe.

"That's..." You're at a complete loss for words. "What *is* that?"

Your co-pilot shakes her head. "Not sure. But whatever it is, that's what the Dauntless was running from." She pauses, then delivers you an ominous look. "Or still is."

There's nothing more to see here. Take the exit and *HEAD TO PAGE 100*

"Forget it," you tell Serena sternly. "And that's an order."

Your co-pilot's eyes are all disappointment, but you can also see she realizes the danger. Clasping her wrist securely you yank her back to her feet.

Together, through the heat and the haze, you make your way to the opposite exit.

Better safe than sorry. Head on *OVER TO PAGE 36*

120

You rack your brain, searching for an answer. But no matter what you do, nothing comes up.

"On second thought never mind," you say. "If there's nothing more we can do here, it's time go to. Let's get back to the Kestrel before those things show up."

You leave the alien boarding vessel behind, smashing the Dauntless's stolen command terminal for good measure. As you do, you can't help but feel the nagging sensation of missed opportunity.

A few twists and turns later, and you're back at the Kestrel. Luck is on your side: it's exactly as you left it.

"Fire her up," you tell Serena as you strap into the pilot's seat. The sickle-shaped mothership still looms through the viewport. "We need to get out of here fast, before that thing figures out we're leaving."

The airlock closes and the docking clamps let go. Everything goes green across your console as Serena gets the engines ready for full burn.

"GO!"

Your entire body is forced into the seat as the Kestrel accelerates through to flank speed. Almost right away, the enemy ship begins firing. Green light fills the cockpit. Bolts of energy fly past, narrowly missing their target. You grit your teeth. It's all you can do...

Suddenly there's an explosion of green and white light. You glance up, and a massive, armored battleship fills your viewscreen from end to end. It's the Blackthorne!

Your radio crackles to life. "Kestrel, this is Commodore Garriott. You're cleared for landing, port-side B-dock. Confirm your approach."

Serena takes over, and your ship runs through its landing cycle. Minutes later you're on deck. Not long after that, you're in the Commodore's office for a full debriefing.

"That ship we just destroyed," the Commodore says gruffly. "What was it?"

"We're not exactly sure," you tell him. "It was following the Dauntless, so we–"

"The Dauntless?"

"Yes sir. The ship we were tasked with investigating."

"Hmmm..." You notice the man's expression looks vaguely troubled. "Well, unfortunately the other ship was consumed in the blast. Unlucky, I suppose. We'll just have to review the data you collected during your time on board."

Serena shoots you an uncomfortable glance. "Uh... data, sir?"

"Yes," the Commodore says simply. "You collected data while you were there, of course. Or at the very least you downloaded the mainframe. Didn't you?"

You sigh mightily. This is going to be a very long debriefing...

Hey, look on the bright side. You're alive. You're home. And you saved the solar system from certain invasion! Your career might've suffered a hit, but all things considered you did a pretty good job in reaching

---

THE END

122

You continue firing at the enemy boarding vessel until your guns are empty. The space around the ship is lit with hundreds of glowing red plasma rounds, each capable of piercing even the toughest armor.

All of them miss.

"What's going on?" Serena cries over the chaos. "I thought you knew how to work this thing?"

There's not even time to argue. The other ship comes around, opens its own cannons, and tears into the Dauntless with two sinister-looking green beams. You watch helplessly as they rip a deadly and devastating line through the hull, eventually tearing your ship clean in half.

The power fails. Everything goes utterly, hopelessly dark. There's nothing to do but wait for the vacuum of space, which, of course, signifies

THE END

The ducts are hot, cramped, and uncomfortable. Even so, they make you feel safe. Sounds float up from below; strange hollow bangs, the hydraulic hiss of pressure doors opening and closing. They're looking for you, you realize. And they're not at all happy.

Serena leads you through the ventilation tubes for quite some time. Eventually she stops, coils a leg back, and kicks out one of the gratings.

You jump back to the deck at one of the Dauntless's Lifeboat stations. The airlock to the escape ship is open before you. It's clean inside. Empty. It's even powered up.

"Not an option," you say, though you know your words aren't needed. "We're taking the Kestrel off this—"

Approaching footsteps halt any further conversation. One of the creatures is pulling itself awkwardly through the corridor. It's heading straight for you.

There's still just enough time to run... maybe. If so, *TURN TO PAGE 24*
You could also hide in the lifeboat, and wait for the creature to pass. If that's the plan, *JUMP TO PAGE 73*

124

The Communications Room comes alive with lights and readouts as Serena works on pulling the Dauntless's flight logs. Anything and everything the ship has done should be here. Where it came from, when it arrived, exactly what it was carrying – all of these things should tell you who ran this ship, and more importantly, where they suddenly disappeared to.

"Nothing."

You blink at Serena in astonishment. "What do you mean nothing?"

"I mean it's all been wiped. Everything. All flight data and communications have been totally erased from the system. Either that, or this is the ship's maiden voyage."

You scan the intricate control surfaces and communications equipment laid out before you. It certainly looks new. Or to be more accurate, it appears... futuristic. You're no expert of course, but the technical aspects seem well past what you've grown accustomed to during your career with the EWC.

"That can't be," you say. "There would at least be information on this flight. Cargo manifests, incoming and outgoing transmission logs. Flight plans..."

"The only thing I can tell you is the ship's radio was set to '99'. Don't know who they'd expect to communicate with like that, because it's a dummy frequency. It's not really used for anything, except–"

Serena is interrupted by the sharp chirp of an alarm. She brings her hand over to tap on a series of buttons, activating a large screen that was previously dark.

126

On the overhead display, the sickle-shaped ship has grown to enormous proportions. It looks wickedly sharp now. Jagged and deadly. Like nothing in the entire solar system.

As you watch, a smaller ship detaches from the larger one. It begins speeding away with an even greater velocity. Your eyes follow it until it disappears off-screen.

"Uhhh... is that thing heading for–"

"Yes," Serena acknowledges. "Looks like we're going to have company."

Three corridors exit the room, each looking pretty much like the others.

If you take the LEFT side corridor, *TURN TO PAGE 129*

If you run down the RIGHT one, *TURN TO PAGE 100*

If you hate left and right that's cool too, just take the center exit and *TURN TO PAGE 53*

"Get DOWN!"

You push Serena to the floor and throw yourself over her a split-second before the room explodes with green light. Fire-suppression systems kick in, sucking the oxygen from the air. Smoke fills the chamber.

"They took out the external array," Serena coughs. "They knew where we were..."

"Correction," you tell her. "Where we *are*."

A few of the video feeds are still up. Through the haze, you can see the creatures moving quickly now, and with renewed purpose. No longer are they searching every room and corridor. They're on their way to you.

"Get up! We've got to go!"

Still coughing, you pull Serena to her feet and point to the exit.

That corridor is looking pretty good right about now.
TURN TO PAGE 107

128

"Wait here," you tell Serena. "And back me up."

Slowly, quietly, you creep into the room. You make so little noise you swear you can hear your heart beating. Your victim doesn't turn, doesn't notice you. At least not yet.

Closer and closer you edge your way forward. Then, when you're only a few feet away, you pounce!

Flying through the air, you throw the full weight of your body into the person seated at the Comm Station. They fall forward, slamming into the controls. The helmet detaches from their environmental suit, then rolls across the floor as you bring one arm up around your unsuspecting victim's neck...

The suit is empty!

The next thing you know Serena is standing over you, laughing harder than you've ever seen her laugh before. She extends one arm. Flushing red with embarrassment you push it away and struggle to your feet without her help.

"Well, what now?" your co-pilot smirks, kicking the helmet. "Should we interrogate him?"

"Whatever." Your humiliation fades quickly though, and you even manage to grin. "Let's check the Dauntless's communication logs."

Hey, at least you didn't need backup. *TURN TO PAGE 124*

The sight of the rapidly-approaching boarding vessel has you rattled. You and Serena are running so fast you hardly notice you've entered a large open area.

It's a gymnasium. The Dauntless's fitness center sports immaculate, state of the art equipment; variable gravity weights, resistance machines, even old school heavy bags for working out your toughest frustrations.

On the other side of the gym a man approaches you. He's dressed in silk boxing trunks and wears thick blue gloves. The man follows your movements, advancing on you even as you sidestep to avoid him. He gets very close to melee range when you finally pull your service pistol.

"Wait!" Serena cries helplessly. She turns toward him. "Who are you? What do you want?"

But the man keeps coming. He's lithe but powerful, muscular but fast. He throws a few quick jabs into the air and you know immediately you're outclassed.

"I'm telling you to stop," you say loudly, leveling the pistol his way. "Last chance."

If you choose to shoot (hey, you warned him) *HEAD DOWN TO PAGE 78*

If you decide to give him a taste of his own medicine, throw your best punch and *FLIP OVER TO PAGE 69*

If you'd rather avoid this guy altogether and duck past him, *TURN TO PAGE 101*

130

You raise your arm up high overhead. Then, after mentally crossing your fingers, you slam down at the monster with all of your might.

Lucky for you, your aim is true. Your weapon blasts down on the creature's unsuspecting, unprotected head, knocking it completely unconscious.

Or at least, it appears to be unconscious.

"Oh wow," Serena breathes, circling the creature in awe. "Look at this thing!"

Dropping the pipe, you move in. Up close the monster appears even more menacing. Jagged rows of spiked teeth line its maw. It doesn't have a snout, but it doesn't exactly not have one either. There are holes in its head where the ears should be, and some form of cartilage built up around them. The entire surface of its reptilian skin seems wet and shiny with some sort of secretion.

"Is that space-mucus?"

"Dunno," you shrug. You're too focused on the creature's claws. So wickedly curved and sharp, you wonder what those claws were meant to rend and tear back on its home world.

The creature stirs slightly, but doesn't wake up.

"Let's go," Serena tells you. "We're wasting ti–"

A crashing sound from behind you ushers you into the next corridor. Something's coming. Again.

Uh oh. Better *FLIP BACK TO PAGE 23*

You squeeze some of the black goo into your mouth (REALLY?) and wince as it dissolves over your tongue. It tastes like meat, vegetables, fish, fruit – all mixed together – simultaneously overwhelming your senses. The best way to describe it is like your taste buds just got punched in the gut.

Serena is looking up at you expectantly. She frowns as you spit the rest out.

"No good?"

"No," you tell her. "It's like jamming all of Thanksgiving in your mouth, all at once." You drop the condensed food tube and the empty coffee bulb as you nod toward the exit.

"Let's get out of here."

Time to go. *TURN TO PAGE 36*

132

The narrow corridor ends in a very large area. It doesn't feel that way however, because the room is filled with consoles, screens, and more wires than you've ever seen in your life.

"The shield emitter," Serena says. She consults a nearby terminal. "It's not online, but..."

You've heard that tone in your co-pilot's voice before. It's never good. "But what?"

"But the plasma injection sequence is still running."

You sigh and roll your eyes at the same time. "And let me guess. That's bad, right?"

"Very."

You notice now the entire area appears to be damaged. Bits of blackened debris are scattered around. It also looks like someone put out a few fires.

Serena pushes a series of buttons and works some slide controls. A board lights up beside you. Three of its buttons are flashing wildly in an alarm sequence; red, yellow, and blue.

Eventually you ask the question. "What can we do?"

"I don't know how to shut it down," your co-pilot tells you. "But it's hot. *Too* hot. We're going to have to jettison the whole plasma injection assembly."

Slowly you close your eyes and count to three. "Or what?" you finally ask.

"Or a good chunk of this ship blows up."

You're about to ask how much time you have when another screen blinks on. Serena suddenly looks hopeful. "Looks like someone was in the process of entering the ejection sequence," she says. "That's good news. But they stopped short of putting in final code."

Together you and your co-pilot squint down at the monitor. But there's a problem. The screen is partially broken and covered in static.

"I can't make out those last two numbers," Serena says. "What do you think they are?"

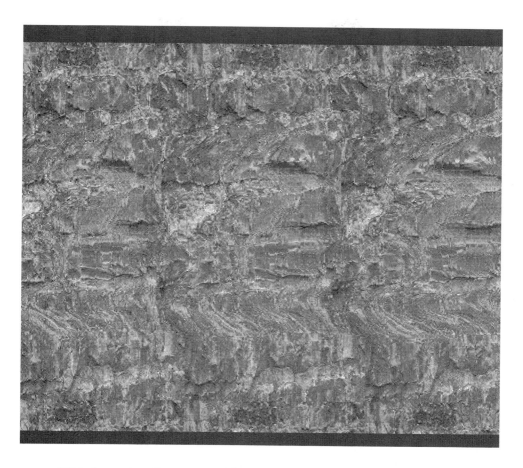

[This image is a **Stereogram**. If you stare at a point *beyond* the image, and slowly unfocus/cross your eyes, a distinct 3D shape should emerge.]

[The best advice would be to relax your eyes. If you can manage to get your vision off focus, at some point you will be able to see the hidden image.]

[Some people can see Stereograms easily. Others can't see them at all. Hopefully you're not one of the latter!]

134

You stare and stare down at the screen as the lights blink rapidly beneath you. Finally Serena leans back.

"I can't see anything!" she cries out in frustration. Your partner digs painfully at her eyes with the backs of two knuckles. "Can you?"

***

If you can make out the two numbers on the broken screen, you're a hero! All you have to do now is *GO TO THAT PAGE*

If you can't see the numbers, that's okay too. You'll just have to pick one of the flashing alarm buttons, and hope it's the one that will complete the sequence!

To press the RED button, *GO TO PAGE 15*

To press the BLUE button, *HEAD TO PAGE 48*

To press the YELLOW button, *FLIP TO PAGE 77*

As silent as you've ever been in your life, you sneak up to within a few feet of the monstrous alien creature. As it bends down to examine a piece of discarded machinery, you pull back and strike!

BIG mistake.

The pipe bounces harmlessly off one of the metal plates fused into the creature's body. The impact flings your hand back, ripping the makeshift weapon from your rattled, trembling fingers.

You don't have time to react as your enemy spins and lashes out at you. A single flick of its massive arm hurls you across the room like a child's doll. You crash into a stack of aluminum pallets with such force you're pretty sure your body left an Andon-shaped indentation.

"Hey! Over here!"

Serena's voice distracts the creature, but only for a second. There's little time to recover. For a heartbeat the monster stands still, perfectly silhouetted against the Dauntless's outer hull. In this single moment of hesitation, you act.

If you pull out your pistol and take a shot, *GO TO PAGE 29*

If you think the rifle would pack more punch, *TURN TO PAGE 114*

136

The next corridor opens into a large circular area. Computer consoles line the walls in a semi-circle, flanked on top by a spectacular array of broad, flat screens.

"Is this the bridge?" Serena asks.

"No. It's not big enough." You touch one of the consoles and buttons light up everywhere. A few of the screens even flash to life. "This is Secondary Command."

Your co-pilot eyes go wide. She nods in agreement. "If you're right, we should be able to control the ship from here."

"Hopefully."

Serena gives you a smirk. "No, not hopefully," she says as she slides into a chair. Her fingers immediately begin working a touch-pad. "Think positive!"

"Fine, then. Definit–"

You're interrupted by a feminine voice that booms down from overhead. "CONSOLE REQUEST INITIATED. COMMAND CODE REQUIRED."

Serena stops typing. Her fingers are frozen mid-keystroke. Her hands look like claws.

"COMMAND CODE REQUIRED."

You glance at each other. "Command code?" you ask. "What's the command code?"

"Not sure we got that," Serena replies. She tilts her head quizzically. "Or did we?"

"COMMAND CODE REQUIRED," the voice repeats for a third time.

"I... I guess I could run an algorithm to take brute force of the console," Serena suggests. "If the system doesn't lock me out first."

Well, do you you have the Command Code? If so, great! Just *TURN TO THAT PAGE*

If you don't know the Command Code, you're left with two other choices:
You can have Serena attempt to seize control of the console *OVER ON PAGE 95*
Or you can leave Secondary Command altogether by *HEADING TO PAGE 100*

You grab the anti-grav handtruck and kick the power on. One of your first jobs as a recruit was running the loading dock on Luna Station. The grips feel instantly familiar in your hands. You know this thing.

The aliens keep coming. Luckily, they're still pretty much together. They might be big, but they're not entirely genius. And that's good.

Surging forward you thumb the overclock safety and accelerate full speed across the Hazardous Cargo deck. There's a scary moment where the spent fuel rod containers seem to leap out at you, but you maneuver deftly around them.

The handtruck slams into the monsters with enough force to double them over. You'd swear you heard the cracking of ribs, but maybe that was your imagination. The truck continues screaming across the bay, its unwilling passengers in tow, until you pass beneath the half-open titanium airlock. Then you leap clear of the platform – with about fifteen feet to spare – and watch as it crashes spectacularly into the outer doors.

You roll to your feet and scramble backwards under the awning. Luckily Serena has taken your lead and is already at the operations terminal. The inner airlock slams shut just as your feet pass the line. Through the wide rectangular porthole you see the monsters writhing furiously, still pinned between the handtruck and the wall.

Serena's hand hovers over the large red button that will gas the outer doors and flush the creatures into space. Gently you close your fingers over her own.

"No," you tell her. "They're bloodthirsty. Doesn't mean we have to be."

Still shaking with adrenaline, the two of you back away from the terminal and head toward the exit.

Very nice work. Now *TURN TO PAGE 64*

138

You enter what could only be called a Rec-room. Game consoles rest beneath wall-flush screens, and a multi-leveled table with strange paddles dominates the center of the room.

On the walls you see framed photos of the Dauntless's crew members in various stages of having fun. Dressed in black and yellow jumpsuits they seem to be smiling and laughing, while Lucite plaques on the wall show scores, records, and accolades.

To your left you notice the source of the light; one control panel still blinks orange, indicating partial power. An old-style arcade game flashes across the screen. Its lights and sounds beckon you to hit the START button.

If you hit that button *FLIP OVER TO PAGE 59*

If you'd rather keep things smooth and by the numbers, exit the room and *TURN TO PAGE 91*

You don't know the bypass code! There's nothing left to do!

ONE SECOND...

In a final act of desperation you draw your service pistol and fire at the computer console. It's Serena's last chance!

Maybe it'll work... maybe it won't. Either way, it's worth a shot. Literally!

Pull out a coin and flip it!

If the coin comes up HEADS, *TURN TO PAGE 80*

If it comes up TAILS instead, *TURN TO PAGE 113*

140

"One four zero!" you blurt out. "The command code is ONE FOUR ZERO, remember?"

Serena types rather than talks. She finishes the code and looks up expectantly.

"CODE ACCEPTED," the voice rings out. "COMMAND ACCESS GRANTED, LEVEL NINE PRIVILEGES."

Serena lets out a huge breath. You smile at her as she slumps forward in relief.

"HAVE A NICE DAY."

You laugh involuntarily. "Level nine!" you tease. "Sounds serious."

"Yeah yeah."

In a matter of minutes your co-pilot is in full command of the Dauntless's data console. Unfortunately however, her victory is short-lived.

"Everything's gone!"

"What?"

"It's like that all over the ship," Serena explains. "Every log, every manifest – it's all erased, or rather, it's like these things never existed at all."

"What about the Deck Cams?" you ask.

Serena looks taken aback. Almost impressed. "I never even thought of that," she says. Then, to herself: "How in the world did I not think of that?" Her fingers fly, and seconds later you're staring upward at a series of viewscreens. This time they're actually filled with people!

"Again," your partner frowns, "almost everything has been erased." She points up at the bank of monitors. "Everything except for this few minutes of trailing footage."

You stand there waiting for the other shoe to drop. "Umm... can we play it?"

Serena punches a large green button. "Oh yeah."

Wanna watch a movie? *TURN TO PAGE 118*

They're too big. And there are too many of them.

You look down at the grenades. The high-explosive one should do it. After all, if you there were ever a situation that called for a high explosive grenade, this is it!

You pull the pins on a pair of them. Then you throw...

Serena is saying something. You can't make out what it is. There's too much confusion, and the corridor is too crowded. A grenade strikes one of the creatures in the foot. It picks it up, what passes for its face registering something that might be even construed as curiosity...

BOOM!

The high-explosive grenade does its job... all too well. It blows out the bulkhead and tears a gaping hole in the hull. You don't even have time to blink before you're sucked out into space, pinwheeling through the void alongside your co-pilot, the creatures, and even their ship.

Hey, at least you stopped them. But for you and Serena, it's pretty obvious this is

THE END

142

You skid backward as the loadbot presses on, intent on slamming you into the nearest container. The momentum forces you to your knees, the robot's arms pushing elbow-deep into the crate as you hold on for dear life.

CLICK!

You glance up at the sound of a switch being thrown. You can barely see past the white-hot glow of the bot's plasma torch as it continues bearing down on you.

CLICK... CLICK... CLICK!

As suddenly as it began its charge, the robot abruptly stops. Its arms go stiff, its body rigid. You hear the fading hiss of hydraulics as it powers down, and when the smoke clears you find Serena clinging tightly – with both arms and legs – to the loadbot's back.

"You're nuts!" she chides you as she climbs down. "Did you really just try to shoot it?"

You grab your co-pilot's outstretched hand and practically hug her to your feet. Still shaking with adrenaline, you make your way from the Cargo hold without another look back.

Whew, that was close! *TURN TO PAGE 66*

SNEAK PEEK

Welcome to the Greensboro City Zoo!

You are KATY RODRIGUEZ, a Corporal in the Greensboro City Police Department. Not only are you one of the city's finest in uniform, but you're the top candidate for promotion to Sergeant next month. You've been working hard, putting in the extra hours, and it's all finally about to pay off.

All you need to do is coast until then, and not screw up.

You leave the small convenience store with two coffees in hand, and climb into the driver side of your police cruiser. "Dude, you got me decaf, right?" asks JERRY HOLMAN, your patrol partner.

"Yes," you say, handing him the cup. He's a good policeman, but a bit of a beach bum. And he whines a lot. "Two sugars, no cream," you add as he opens his mouth to ask. "And don't call me dude!"

His mouth closes and he nods thankfully. "Why are you drinking the strong stuff?" he asks, glancing at his watch. "We've only got an hour until shift's over."

"I'm hoping to catch the second half of the game," you say, testing the temperature of the coffee. The Greensboro Gryphons are two games from making the playoffs, and this will be one of the few nights you get home in time to see any of the game.

Jerry shrugs. "Me, I'm going to get some much needed sleep."

"All you do is sleep," you tease.

"Hey, some of us enjoy a rest. We can't all bust our butts to make Sergeant!"

You think of another joke, but bite it back. You *have* been busting your butt, and it's nice to hear someone say so.

Suddenly your radio crackles to life. "Unit 41. Unit 41. Come in."

Uh oh. That's you.

You move your coffee to your other hand and grab the radio receiver. "This is Unit 41, over."

"Please hold for Captain Beckett." The radio goes silent.

You share a look with Jerry. Captain Beckett? It's rare for one of the station chiefs to get on the dispatch radio.

The speaker hisses with static before the Captain's voice sounds. "Officer Rodriguez? Officer Holman?"

"We're here, Captain."

"Good, good, uhh..." he pauses to take a deep breath. "There's a disturbance at the Greensboro City Zoo. I need you to take a look."

Jerry groans.

"Sir," you say, "we're six miles from there. Surely there's a patrol that's closer."

"I trust you with this, Rodriguez," he says gruffly. "Are you saying you can't handle it?"

"Of course not, sir," you quickly say. "What kind of disturbance?"

There's a long pause on the radio. "Our details are fuzzy. They'll tell you when you get there."

"*But we get off in an hour,*" Jerry whispers.

You hold a finger up to shush him. "Roger that Captain," you say.

"I'm counting on you, Rodriguez," Captain Beckett says ominously.

You and Jerry sit there for a few quiet moments.

"There goes my extra sleep," Jerry mutters.

"Oh quit whining," you say. "We'll pop over there and take care of it in a pinch."

Jerry takes the coffee from your hand. "Well then you'd better give me the strong stuff."

145

The police sirens wails and flashes as you wind through the city. Five minutes later you're whizzing past the "Welcome to the Greensboro City Zoo" sign and screeching to a stop in the parking lot.

You and Jerry climb out of the car simultaneously. Although it's well past the zoo's closing hours, the massive metal gates stand wide open. A few pieces of paper blow through the opening.

"That's weird," Jerry says.

You nod. You've got a strange feeling about this.

Your boots crunch along the pavement as you approach. A flock of colorful birds flutter into the air as you pass through the gates and into the zoo walkway, but nothing scarier than that. Ahead of you is the Visitor Center, where tickets and souvenirs are sold. There's some sort of red light on inside the window. A shadow passes in front of it.

Involuntarily, your hand touches your pistol holster. "Who's there!" you call out. "This is the Greensboro Police Department!"

The man steps out from the building. In the moonlight you see that he's young, like an intern, wearing a zoo uniform with green suspenders. "Oh thank goodness you're here," he says, frantic. "I'm not cut out for this. Way above my skill level."

You relax. "Calm down. Can you tell us what's going on?"

"I've gotta get out of here," he says, pushing past you.

"Hey, wait!" Jerry yells as the intern makes a break for the entrance.

"You're safe with us," you add. "We're trained officers with weapons."

"You're going to need more than that!" the intern yells. "There's tranquilizer rifles in the Warden's Hut, if you can get there!" And with that he disappears into the darkness.

You glance at Jerry. He's too stunned to speak.

The lights are off in the Visitor Center, and you realize that reddish glow was an emergency light over the doorway. "Looks like the power is out," you say.

Jerry points. "The door to the employee office is in the corner."

You head over to the door, which has, "Employees Only" printed in big yellow letters. There's an electric keypad next to the door, with numbers 1-9 glowing. There must be a backup generator to keep the emergency systems online.

Thankfully the door is wide open, so you slip inside.

There are desks and file cabinets filled with papers. The only illumination comes from another emergency light above the doorway, and a single computer screen across the room.

Jerry grabs a medical kit from the desk. "Why's that computer on?"

"Must be on the backup circuit"" you say, stepping up to it. There's an email open:

Dave, as the only member of the night crew it's imperative that you get the systems back online. Get to the Maintenance Shed and enable the backup power. If you need protection from Project Fusion then retrieve a tranq rifle from the Warden Hut. You know the code.
- Warden Oxford

And a response:

Respectfully, sir: you're out of your mind! I'm not trained for that kind of work, and it would only make her ANGRY! I've called the police. Let them take care of it. I'm getting out of here.
- Dave

"Huh," Jerry says after reading. "What's Project Fusion?"

You shake your head. "I don't know, but it sounds dangerous. It's a good thing you grabbed that medical kit. We'd better call the Captain."

The phones are down–which is probably why the intern used email to communicate–but thankfully you've got your radio. "Dispatch, this is officer Rodriguez, over."

A few minutes later and you're connected to the Captain. "Huh?" he asks.

"Sir, the place is deserted. The only night employee just ran away like he'd seen a ghost! The power is out too." You quickly fill him in on the details of the email.

Captain Beckett clears his throat when you finish. "Well..."

Suddenly there is a rumble outside. You and Jerry run to the window just in time to see a huge, hulking shape. As it comes into view the moonlight glistens off two long, ivory tusks.

An elephant!

You watch in stunned silence as it lumbers past and walks out the gate, into the street. "Duuude..." whispers Jerry.

"And I think the animals are loose," you add to the radio. "I'm officially requesting backup. We need animal control in here."

The Captain sighs. "Okay, I'm going to be straight with you, Rodriguez. Warden Oxford is an old friend of mine, and he needs our help. We've already contacted animal control, but they won't be there for two hours. I need to you to do whatever cleanup you can until then. Try to contain as many of the animals as you can. And close those gates, so no more animals get out! I don't know why the power is out, but figure it out."

"But sir, we're not qualified for this sort of thing."

"If you take care of this," he adds, "that promotion is as good as yours. If you don't... well. Carry on then. And oh, make sure you don't harm any of the animals."

"What?" Jerry blurts out.

"I'm serious, Holman. Lock your sidearm in the police cruiser, so you're not tempted to use it. Injured animals are a PR nightmare. Understood?"

"Yessir."

The radio goes silent.

"Well then." You unholster your sidearm and hand it to Jerry. "Put 'em away."

He stares, dumbfounded. "You can't be serious."

"It was a direct order. We still have our pepper spray. Go ahead, I'll stay here and look around."

After he grumbles and heads back to the car, you look around the Visitor Center. There's a stack of maps on the check-out counter, and you unfold one and take a look.

"Looks like we have a lot of ground to cover," you tell Jerry when he gets back. "Let's get to it."

You pass through the turnstiles and into the zoo grounds. With the power off, the path that winds through the park is dark and ominous. You pull out your flashlight and cast a cone of light before you. With the way the shadows play you're still unnerved, and the fingers of your free hand itch to grab the pepper spray from your belt. Jerry is unusually quiet, so he must feel the same.

To steady yourself, you stop to read one of the informational signs along the path:

*When defending yourself from a bear attack, the species of bear will determine the best course of action. If attacked by a **Black Bear**, fight back by striking the bear in the head and face. **Grizzly Bears** are not so timid, however, so the best course of action is to fall to the ground in the fetal position and play dead.*

Jerry is stopped at the next sign ahead of you, doing the same. That one is about snakes:

*The **Coral Snake** and **King Snake** look similar, but don't be fooled! **Coral Snakes** are venomous, while **King Snakes** are harmless. To remember the difference, remember the rhyme: If red touches black, it's safe for Jack. If red touches yellow, it kills the fellow.*

Jerry swallows audibly. "We're not going to have to deal with snakes, are we?"

"I don't know."

"Because I'm not a biologist, or a snakeologist, or whatever it's called that—"

You cut him off. "Come on. Let's keep moving. The path splits up ahead."

149

The sound of splashing water greets you as you enter a wide pavilion. In the center is a stone fountain spraying water over the edge. The falling mist looks strange in the light of your flashlight. "But if the electricity is out," you say, "then what's powering the pump?"

Jerry points. "I don't think that's the pump causing that..."

Without warning, a brown antelope leaps out of the fountain. It lands on the ground and teeters on unsteady legs, the hooves slipping wetly on the pavement. When it regains its balance it stares directly at you, flicks its ears, and then bolts.

Three more antelope bound out of the fountain to follow, leaving a trail of water leading into the woods. The sound of rustling trees slowly fades.

"Well," you say, "it's better than snakes. Right?"

Jerry mumbles something incoherent.

You approach the fountain. Rising out of the center is a signpost with ten arrows pointing in different directions. "The Warden's email said we need to turn the power on."

"It also said," Jerry points out, "that we should grab tranquilizer rifles from the Warden Hut if we need protection from Project Fusion."

"We don't even know what Project Fusion is."

Jerry nods vigorously. "Exactly!"

The arrow for the Maintenance Shed points to the left. The arrow for the Warden Hut points to the right.

Which way will *you* go when you try to solve the...

ENIGMA
AT THE
GREENSBORO ZOO

ABOUT THE AUTHORS

Danny McAleese started writing fantasy fiction during the golden age of Dungeons & Dragons, way back in the heady, adventure-filled days of the 1980's. His short stories, The Exit, and Momentum, made him the Grand Prize winner of Blizzard Entertainment's 2011 Global Fiction Writing contest.

He currently lives in NY, along with his wife, four children, three dogs, and a whole lot of chaos. www.dannymcaleese.com

David Kristoph lives in Virginia with his wonderful wife and two not-quite German Shepherds. He's a fantastic reader, great videogamer, good chess player, average cyclist, and mediocre runner. He's also a member of the Planetary Society, patron of StarTalk Radio, amateur astronomer and general space enthusiast. He writes mostly Science Fiction and Fantasy. www.DavidKristoph.com